MURDERING WELLS

Military deserters rob a mail contractor and leave him to the mercy
of Apache raiders in a remote corner
of Arizona. The contractor's brother,
Luke Adison, vows to track down
those responsible. Soon the tables
turn, however, as Luke is captured
by the deserters. Will he manage to
escape and avenge his brother — or
will he learn the true secret behind
the sinisterly named Murdering
Wells?

GREG MITCHELL

◆

MURDERING WELLS

Complete and Unabridged

LINFORD
Leicester

First published in Great Britain in 2010 by
Robert Hale Limited
London

First Linford Edition
published 2011
by arrangement with
Robert Hale Limited
London

The moral right of the author has been asserted

British Library CIP Data

Mitchell, Greg, *1935* –
   Murdering Wells. - - (Linford western library)
   1. Revenge- -Fiction. 2. Brothers- -Fiction.
   3. Western stories. 4. Large type books.
   I. Title II. Series
   823.9′2–dc22

   ISBN 978–1–4448–0762–2

Published by
F. A. Thorpe (Publishing)
Anstey, Leicestershire

Set by Words & Graphics Ltd.
Anstey, Leicestershire
Printed and bound in Great Britain by
T. J. International Ltd., Padstow, Cornwall

1

Matt Adison knew he was in trouble when his four-man cavalry escort deserted him, stole his buckboard with the mailbags and left him stranded in the Arizona desert. Twelve miles lay between him and the closest settlement in country where a five-mile walk in the heat could prove too much for many people.

At first he was more angry than fearful, confident that he knew enough about desert travel to survive. The real fear came when he discovered that the Apaches were stalking him. Adison was not sure when they had first arrived on the scene because visibility was limited in the jumble of boulders and cactus where he had sought refuge from the midday sun. It was the bird-calls at a time when most animals and birds were not stirring that alerted him. One bird was near the road that he had left when seeking the shade. His tracks would be visible there. Another was closer, by the sound of it, only about fifty yards away. Two Apaches were more than enough to handle but he knew that there were probably others. The military had been looking for a small band of about half a dozen warriors.

Adison was not totally defenceless. The deserters had taken his Colt revolver but had overlooked the small, four-barrelled Sharps .32 he had concealed as a hideout gun. It would not be much use against well-armed Apache raiders but it was all he had. Fearing even to guess about the odds against his survival, he could only clutch the little pistol and hope for a miracle.

Something stirred the tops of weeds barely ten paces from where he was crouched. No wind was blowing and Adison had no doubt that something living and potentially deadly was concealed there. With hope fading, the hunted man knew that the hunters had found his hiding place. A bird called from somewhere over to his right. At least three warriors were stalking him. No reply came from the man in the weeds because he knew that he was close to his prey.

Then, out of the corner of his eye, Adison saw another Apache warrior appear from behind a tall patch of cactus. He seemed to just glide into view, a small dark man with a red rag tied around his long, black hair. He wore a ragged, grey shirt, a breech clout, and the long moccasins of the desert Apache. A Winchester carbine was held at hip level and the warrior's eyes darted about, seeking a target. Then the hunter's gaze settled on the white man crouching in the shade of a boulder, only partly concealed behind a greasewood bush. A wild yell broke from the Apache's lips and the muzzle of the Winchester swung towards its intended target.

Adison fired quickly. The little pistol

barked spitefully but the bullet it spat missed its mark. Though the warrior immediately dropped behind a boulder, the white man knew that his shot had been wasted. The Sharps was not designed for ranges greater than a couple of feet and a tiny pistol in a big hand was not a recipe for accuracy.

The Apache in the weeds jumped to his feet with a blood-chilling shout and levelled a carbine at his opponent. Both men fired at once.

A hammer blow knocked Adison's right leg from under him and stretched him on his back on the ground. The Apache appeared to be slightly wounded but was still on his feet. Another shot came from the side and narrowly missed the white man. Adison rolled over to see two more warriors appear from the brush. With two shots left, he snapped one at the nearest Apache with no apparent result. The last shot, he fired into his own brain.

★ ★ ★

Luke Adison halted outside the single-storey adobe building that was the temporary headquarters of Captain Guthrie's cavalry detachment in Yucca Springs. Since the latest Apache outbreak, the captain's men had been providing escorts to travellers on the forty miles of road between that town and Shelbyville. He stood there a moment, a wiry, dark-haired young man in dusty clothes with a week's dark stubble on his deeply tanned face. He was trying to gather his thoughts, for he had many questions to ask. The telegram announcing his brother's death had not told him much.

A soldier with a carbine in his arms was standing in the shade just inside the doorway. He pulled himself into a slightly more military posture when he saw that Adison was approaching. 'Is there something I can do for you, mister?'

'Yes. I'm Luke Adison. I was told to see Captain Guthrie about my brother's murder.'

The sentry called to someone inside. 'I have a civilian here — name's Adison — wants to see Captain Guthrie about a murder.'

Another soldier appeared, a slightly tidier version of the sentry. 'The captain got your telegraph message and is expecting you. Just follow me.'

Guthrie was seated behind a paper-cluttered table that did duty for an office desk. His thin face with its large moustache was that of a worried man and premature baldness had made him appear older than his forty years. He rose, shook hands with Adison, indicated a straight-backed chair in front of his desk and asked, 'What can I do for you Mr Adison?'

'I understand, Captain, that you led the search party that found my brother's remains after he was killed by the Apaches a couple of months ago.'

'That's right. He had the mail contract between here and the army post at Camp Grant. When he was overdue, I took out a patrol. We found your brother's body. Strictly speaking the Indians did not kill him. But he was in a position where he had no chance of escape because of a wound. He knew enough to shoot himself rather than fall alive into Apache hands. He's buried here in the local cemetery.'

'There's something I don't understand,' Luke said. 'From what Matt told me in previous letters, he had an armed escort whenever the Apaches were causing trouble and he always carried a six-shooter himself. The mail trip should have been fairly safe. What went wrong?'

Guthrie looked uncomfortable. For a second he looked nervously at the low ceiling as if seeking inspiration from there. Then he said slowly, 'The escort deserted and left your brother stranded. They stole the mail and went through it looking for money. We found it a few miles from where your brother died.'

This latest revelation hit Luke like a physical blow. For a second or two he was silent, but then he said angrily,

'That's the first I've heard of this but I knew something was mighty odd. Have you caught those deserters?'

'We haven't yet — but we will. The army is after them for desertion and the civil government is chasing them for mail robbery. We'll get them.'

Luke was not convinced. 'So far no one seems to have done much good. They've been gone for two months now. Tell me who they are and what they look like and I'll have a damn good try at tracking them down.'

'I'm afraid you would not find them. We have trained lawmen on the job. This is not a task for amateurs.'

'I've had a bit of practice. I'm currently on leave from the Texas Rangers. Just tell me who I'm looking for.'

'I'm afraid I can't do that. This matter is part of a major investigation into the theft of military property. Desertion is a big problem and deserters sometimes sell military equipment to raise money. Some characters are actually encouraging men to desert and are making a good living turning over stolen horses and guns as well as selling civilian clothes to the deserters and even charging them to hide out. There is a big investigation under way and we don't want outsiders interfering. I know how you feel but I cannot disclose any names. The men who deserted your brother would be using other names by now.' Guthrie shrugged his shoulders. 'I'd like to help but I have my orders. I must warn you, though. Don't get involved and hamper any government investigations.'

Luke stood up and extended a hand. 'Thanks for what you did for my brother, Captain. I'll have a look at Matt's grave and then hang around town for a while, figuring out my next move. This is my first venture into Arizona and I might have a look around before heading back to Texas.'

The worried look returned to Guthrie's face. 'I hope you took notice of what I said, Mr Adison. Don't try to interfere in this matter because it is far more complicated than it looks.'

'I can see that,' Luke told him as he walked to the door. 'Uncle Sam won't need to worry about me being underfoot.'

'That's good to hear. I hope you have a pleasant stay in the territory here and a safe journey back to Texas. Remember what I said though, leave this matter to the professionals.'

'Thanks for the advice. I'll remember what you said.'

'Remembering is not good enough. Do what I say and save yourself a whole lot of trouble.'

As his visitor left the room Guthrie slumped in his chair. The hard-looking young man's attitude was telling him that his advice would quickly be ignored.

2

Luke knew that the town's two saloons would be a good place to start his quest. He hit pay dirt at the second one, the Cactus Flower. The young barman who served his beer stared rather pointedly at the Colt revolver on Luke's hip. It had an intricately carved ivory butt. Many a Westerner paid extra to have his Colt's wooden butt replaced by a more exotic one and some came from the factory with carved designs, but Luke's gun was one of a pair. An old German gunsmith in a small Texas town had converted a pair of percussion Army Colts to take the new metallic cartridges. He had shortened the barrels and treated all metal parts to a rich blueing process before adding the grips, which he had carved himself. They were a beautiful pair that the gunsmith was not prepared to split.

11

Neither of the two Adison brothers could afford to buy the pair so they had pooled their money, bought the two guns and kept one each.

'That's a nice-looking gun you have there,' the bartender said. He was a thin young man with a serious face and sharp observant eyes. With feigned casual interest, he asked, 'Did you buy that around here somewhere?'

Luke saw that there was a purpose behind the seemingly innocent question and chose carefully the words of his reply. 'No. This one was specially prettied up in Texas. You won't see one like that around here.'

The bartender disagreed. 'I saw one a hell of a lot like that in this very bar. It belonged to a mail contractor named Matt Adison. The Apaches killed him.'

'You knew Matt Adison?'

'Sure did. That's why I'm mighty curious about that gun. I didn't think there was another like it around.'

'I'm Luke Adison, Matt's younger brother. We bought this pair of guns between us and took one each. You should be careful, though. If I had illegally got hold of Matt's gun, you could have had a hole in your hide by now.'

The bartender looked embarrassed. 'I hadn't thought of that. I was just so surprised to see what I thought was Matt's gun. I'm Harry Petersen. Matt used to drink here regularly. It was a hell of a shame what happened to him. Tom Pierce and the others will have a lot to answer for when the army catches up with them.'

Luke's drink stopped halfway to his mouth. 'You knew the men who deserted him?'

'The escort troopers changed regularly but they often had a drink here while waiting for the mail to leave. Sometimes they played a bit of cards. Most of the regulars here got to know the troopers from the various escorts.'

'Do you know who the others were?'

Preston thought a while. 'Fitz was one of them. I don't think we ever heard his full name. He was a noisy little drunk with untidy fair hair. His friends managed to keep him out of trouble but he was a nuisance with a few drinks aboard.'

'What did Pierce look like?'

'Fairly ordinary, thirty at the most with dark hair. His nose looked like it had been busted a time or two. He had an Eastern accent like a New Yorker. That's about all. Wait a minute. He had a small white spot in the hair on the back of his head, probably an old scar.'

'What about the other two?'

'I'm not sure but I'll ask Gus Douglas when he comes in later. Gus is a gambler and played a lot of poker with the escort troopers at different times. He might remember. Are you staying in town?'

'That's right. I have a room at Cowdrey's Hotel. I expect to be here for a couple more days. I'd appreciate it if you would make some enquiries about the others or if you could put me on to someone with a bit more information. I'd be prepared to pay you for your time.'

Petersen waved a hand dismissively. 'Forget it. Matt had a lot of friends around here. Come back tomorrow night and I'll try to have something useful for you.'

Luke returned to his hotel room, his elation tinged with suspicion. He had never expected that he would pick up such vital information so easily. Was it all a bit too easy?

He had two names and rough descriptions and the prospects of getting another couple of names sounded good. Then there was the matter of the gun. If it had fallen into Apache hands it might never show up. However, if the deserters had taken it — and he suspected they would have, it was likely still to be in the territory. Arizona covered a large area but the population was scattered thinly, thanks to the Apache wars only a couple of years previously. In a place where people for miles around all knew each other, they remembered strangers and his brother's gun would surely be noticed.

Next morning he visited the town cemetery. Matt's grave was the most recent and the army had marked it with a headboard that was temporary but substantial enough to last for a couple of years. Luke resolved to replace it with something more appropriate when his quest was over. As he stood by the mound of raw red earth in that desolate place he tried to mutter some half-remembered prayers, but the present kept intruding on his attempts to connect with the hereafter. Feelings of anger and the desire for revenge seemed to override his grief. 'I'll get them, Matt,' he promised. 'I'll get every last one of them.'

The cemetery was not far from town and rather than disturb his horse's rest after the long ride from Texas, he had left it in the livery stable and walked out. He knew that the horse would get plenty of work before long.

As Luke was walking past the livery

stable he saw a man and a woman entering it. The man was tall and broad-shouldered with a handsome face and a small, neatly trimmed moustache. He was dressed in town clothes but wore a wide-brimmed, brown hat and the bulge of a shoulder-holstered revolver showed under his coat.

The woman was stunning, young and shapely with curly blond hair. She wore a stylish riding-habit that was more suited to a park in a big city than a dusty street in Arizona. Luke did not like to stare but glanced again at the couple before they disappeared into the gloom of the big stable. There is one lucky man, he told himself.

Aware that he would not find his men in the town, Luke started restocking his supplies for what he expected would be a long ride. His first task was to locate a source of jerked beef. The dried meat was light to carry and sustaining but was not made commercially. In many towns, though, Mexican and Indian women sometimes sold jerky and Yucca Springs was no exception. After making enquiries he found himself at a small adobe shack where a wrinkled Mexican lady was supervising strips of meat arranged on a rack and drying in the hot sun. A small, smoky fire below kept flies and insects away from the meat.

After a brief discussion in broken English and Spanish, the woman brought out a large biscuit tin filled with jerky that she had already made. Luke purchased enough to last him a week if it had to and with his purchase wrapped in newspaper, paid the seller and left. The price was so reasonable that he knew the meat was probably from some ancient, rangy longhorn, but it did not matter. Tough or tender, the beef was all the same when turned into jerky.

Returning to his hotel room, he checked through his belongings to see if he needed anything else before leaving town. Though he had nearly a full box of cartridges for his Winchester .44 rim-fire carbine, he decided that another box might prove useful given the expected future circumstances. Luke visited the general store and added a couple of cans of sardines and some beans to his purchases as well as the ammunition. Canned food was heavy to carry but sometimes, when camped away from towns, it made cooking much simpler.

As he walked back to the hotel he passed the couple he had seen earlier at the livery stable. They did not seem to notice him and the girl's face wore a frown. 'I don't like that sidesaddle,' Luke heard her complain. 'I'll get myself some pants and ride in a man's saddle.'

'That's hardly ladylike, Gloria,' her companion said. 'Let's go to the store and see if they have a divided skirt you could buy. Or maybe there is a seamstress here who could make one up for you.'

'We don't have time for clothes to be made. The sooner we find Billy, the better. If this store doesn't have a skirt I'm leaving this town on a man's saddle in britches and I don't care what people think.'

Luke smiled to himself and sympathized with the girl. He did not like to see women in sidesaddles. They were hard on horses' backs and too many women had been trapped in them and killed or injured when horses fell.

He looked in at the livery stable to check on his buckskin gelding and packmule. Both looked well-fed and rested. He purchased half a sack of oats from the stableman as emergency rations if he was forced to camp where there was no grazing. He also paid his bill in readiness for an early morning start. As he was about to leave, he remembered Captain Guthrie's comment about the high rate of desertion. Probably the most valuable thing a deserter could sell was his horse. Reputable dealers would not touch government stock except under strict conditions but in Arizona there were many who would make a dollar any way they could.

Feigning ignorance Luke asked, 'Did you ever think of buying cast army horses to rent out? Some of those I've seen looked pretty good, and they were cheap to buy.'

The livery man shook his head. 'Any horses unsuitable for troop work are kept for light work around the post if they are any good. Those that are cast and go straight on to the civilian market are worn out, but even then, there's a lot of paper work needs to be done before the army will brand that bar through the US brand.'

'Too bad.' Luke tried a speculative lie. 'I heard there was someone around these parts who was selling some pretty good ex-army horses.'

'I heard about Josh Coterill too,' the man told him. 'If stories are right you can buy anything from cavalry horses to cannons from that trading post of his at Duncan's Creek. But the army has checked up on him a couple of times and found nothing wrong. It's just another story going round.'

Back in his hotel room Luke added another name and place to his note-book.

3

Luke waited until late to return to the saloon. He knew that Petersen would be busy early in the night. There would be less demand for the bartender's services when the early-rising men from the nearby ranches had departed. He wanted as few interruptions as possible and upon entering the bar found that he had timed things right. A few poker-players were seated at a table in one corner of the room and Petersen was leaning on the bar with an expression of utter boredom on his face.

'Having a quiet night, Harry?'

'Sure am. As soon as that crew in the corner get sick of losing money and go home, I intend to close for the night.'

Luke leaned closer. 'Did you have any luck with those names?'

Petersen looked around to be sure

they were not being overheard. 'I did. One was called Sandy, a young, baby-faced character, and the other was Alan Hallam, medium size with dark hair and a big moustache, in his thirties, Gus thought.'

Luke committed the names and descriptions to memory. He would write them down later in his hotel room. He ordered a beer, and as it was set before him Petersen made another comment. 'It seems everyone wants to catch up with those four. You're not the only one asking about them.'

'I can understand that the army and the law want them pretty badly but they would already know what you just told me.'

'Gus Douglas told me that a dude with a New York accent approached him. He sure isn't the law because he had his sister in tow. Gus said she was a real honey.'

'I think I know the couple you mean,' Luke told him. 'I saw them today. They were arguing about a sidesaddle. I wonder what their interest is in this? Does Gus know anything else about them?'

Preston wiped a cloth through some spilt beer on the bar and replied, 'They hinted that they were kin to one of the deserters and were looking for him. They said they had reason to believe that he might have been forced into what he did.'

Luke felt that such a situation was unlikely and thought no more of the couple. He had his own ideas and sipped his beer before asking, 'Is there a land titles office in this town?'

'No. The nearest is at Copper Rocks about fifteen miles east of here. Are you thinking of a homestead, or a mining claim?'

'Something like that,' Luke said vaguely.

The bartender took the hint and asked no more questions.

Luke thanked him for his assistance and left after finishing his beer. He intended to make an early start in the morning.

His buckskin horse and packmule

were fed and ready to go when he arrived at the stables. Luke had been packing saddles from the time he was tall enough to do so and it did not take him long to saddle both animals. After their confinement in the stables, they seemed eager to be on the road again. There was no need to lead the mule, he had travelled many miles with the horse and followed like a dog.

It was good to be leaving the town and Luke's spirits lifted considerably as the cluster of faded weatherboard-and-adobe buildings receded into the distance. The trail wound through arid red country with mesquite on the flats and various forms of cactus and prickly pear on the slopes. Some high points were bare red rock but others had a crown of dark-green Joshua trees. In places the landscape appeared open but in other areas jumbles of huge boulders crowded the trail's edge. Luke could well imagine why the Apaches, only a few years previously, had set so many ambushes on that stretch of road.

He estimated that his journey was half over when he reached a spot on a hill top partially shaded by some tall boulders and decided that a few minutes' rest would not hurt his animals. Glancing back the way he had come, Luke was surprised to see a rider coming down the trail. At first he thought the man was following his tracks but as he came closer he saw that the rider occasionally twisted in his saddle and looked over his shoulder. Then, at a slight bend in the trail, the stranger halted. When he left the road and concealed himself and his horse among some tall mesquite growing nearby, Luke knew that the newcomer was up to no good.

Two dots appeared from around a distant bend in the trail; these materialized into a pair of riders. The hidden man saw them and sunlight flashed on metal as he drew a carbine from its saddle scabbard.

Luke knew that he was seeing a man preparing to stage what could be a robbery or even a murder.

The oncoming riders were already in rifle range but the man lurking by the roadside would not risk a long shot. In another minute he would not need to do so as his intended victims would be in point-blank range.

Luke quickly untied the halter shank from the mule's neck and fastened it again to the nearest clump of mesquite. The animal was well-trained and he knew that it would stand despite the weak fastening. He mounted the buckskin, drew his carbine from the horn loop and quietly rode back down the slope towards the lurking gunman. The ambusher, with his attention fixed on the approaching riders, had no idea that Luke was behind him.

Just short of the hidden stranger, the two riders saw Luke approaching and, alarmed by the rifle he carried, momentarily checked their horses.

Ignorant of the danger behind him but thinking he had somehow been detected, the gunman spurred his mount from cover, a carbine held pistol-fashion in his right hand. Uncertain whether the man intended robbery or murder or even both, Luke knew that he would have to act quickly.

'Drop your gun,' he called loudly as he suddenly rushed his mount at the man on the trail before him.

Completely surprised, the gunman swung his wiry little pony around. The nearer of the other two riders, a tall man on a sorrel horse, reacted with unexpected speed. He drew a revolver from under his coat and fired at the confused man who now only sought to escape. Luke thought he saw dust fly from the would-be bandit's vest and the man momentarily swayed in the saddle. Then he brought his pony around and charged straight at him. As he came, the Spencer carbine in his hand spat noise and smoke. The shot was hasty and missed its mark. A bullet from a heavy .50-calibre carbine fired one-handed from a galloping horse had little chance of hitting the intended target.

Steadying the fore-grip of his Winchester in the crook of his bridle arm, Luke slammed the butt into his shoulder and fired instinctively. His opponent somersaulted back over his mount's rump and hit the ground in a cloud of red dust. Reining his mount back on its haunches, Luke came out of the saddle, levering another cartridge into his rifle's firing chamber as he dismounted.

'Don't move,' he ordered the man who lay stirring feebly on the ground. The Spencer lay nearby but the wounded man had lost all interest in it. His breath was rasping and it did not take medical qualifications to see that he was dying. He had been struck once in the chest and once in the side and blood was pouring from both wounds as well as coming in frothy bubbles from his lips.

As he knelt by the fallen bandit, Luke saw at a glance a few remnants of military equipment. Acting on a hunch, he asked, 'Where are the others?'

The man's eyes opened as if in surprise, then he gasped, 'They kicked me out . . . goin' to murderin' . . . murderin' . . . '

'Going where?' Luke asked urgently. But he was too late. The man was dead.

'He can't hear you now.' The tall stranger had dismounted and calmly reloaded the fired chamber of his small .38 revolver. Luke turned around and saw the couple he had last seen in town, the ones he had heard were on a similar quest to himself but not for the same reasons.

The blonde girl remained mounted holding the man's horse. The stylish habit was gone and she now wore a divided skirt and bestrode a man's saddle. She looked a little pale but under the circumstances that was understandable.

'I think that my sister and I owe you our thanks,' the man said.

4

'I'm Walt Hammond and this is my sister, Gloria. You came just at the right time. I think that man meant to kill us.'

Luke tipped his hat to the girl and took the man's hand. 'I'm Luke Adison. Sorry you had to see that, Miss Hammond. I didn't want to kill him but he gave me no choice.'

'Why would he be after us?' Walt asked.

'Can't say for sure, but he looks like an army deserter down on his luck and maybe was trying his hand at robbery.'

The Hammonds looked briefly at each other. 'How can you be sure?' Walt asked. 'He looks like a civilian to me.'

Luke pointed to the man's feet. 'He's wearing Jefferson boots and those small, brass spurs are cavalry issue. Some cavalry regiments are still using Spencer repeaters too and I think that if you look at that rifle over there, you'll see army markings stamped on the butt.'

'It sounded as though he was accusing us of murdering him,' Gloria said and shuddered. 'That poor man's troubles were all of his own making.'

Luke started to search the dead man's pockets. 'He won't have anything of value,' he explained to the others, 'but we might be able to find out who he was.' Glancing around he saw the man's pony standing a short distance away trapped by the long rein upon which it was standing. 'You could catch that pony, Walt. He might have something rolled in that blanket behind the saddle. We'll need it anyway to take his body to town.'

Gloria looked a little perturbed. 'Do we have to take the body with us? The man's dead. Shouldn't we just tell the sheriff at the next town?'

'I'm afraid not. The buzzards might make a mess of this man before anyone comes back. It's important that the army is able to recognize him. Walt's coming now with his horse. If he'll help me lift the body across it, I'll wait for a while so you can ride to town ahead of me. That way you won't attract any unfavourable notice when you arrive.'

She flashed a pretty smile. 'That's very thoughtful of you, Luke. I don't like attracting too much attention.'

Luke observed, 'If you don't mind me saying so, Miss Hammond, you'll attract attention around these parts for sure.'

Walt looked doubtfully at the sorry-looking pony with its worn-out, cheap Mexican saddle. He expressed the opinion that a cavalry deserter would normally be better mounted. But Luke had seen similar cases before.

He explained. 'This man probably traded in his cavalry horse and six-shooter for the civilian outfit he has. There are plenty of human buzzards out there who will take advantage of a man on the run. They know how to make a profit out of military horses and guns. Desertion from the army is at such a high rate that it has started a whole new area of criminal activity. I have heard of military posts that lost thirty per cent of their men through desertion. It's mighty easy to get disillusioned with a soldier's life on the frontier.'

Gloria looked slightly embarrassed before telling Luke: 'Walt and I are actually looking for a deserter — our brother Billy. He deserted from the cavalry near here about two months ago. We don't know why. He seemed reasonably content in the army and it is strange that he would suddenly desert. His letters hinted that he might have been coerced by someone else. We are trying to find him before the law does.'

Luke tried not to show the excitement he felt. The man on the ground fitted the description of the soldier known as Fitz and if he was still in the area the others could be too. The Hammonds were a complication, for they were on a similar quest to himself.

The difference was that they were seeking to aid a deserter, but he probably intended to kill the same man. Billy Hammond seemed to have deserted around the same time as Matt was killed although the name did not match those given by Petersen. Had Billy Hammond enlisted under an alias? Sometimes military recruiters did not look too deeply into a man's past. Did the Hammonds have important information that he did not? Judging by dates and places, it seemed likely that their brother was one of the men Luke sought. The problem however, was to learn what the others had found out without arousing their suspicions.

He decided that he would stick close to the pair and try to ascertain what they really knew. But he could not tell them that he was on a mission of vengeance. Luke hated lying to decent people but in his mind he started to concoct a reason for being where he was.

With Walt's help he managed to get the dead man across his saddle and secured him there with a rope.

'How far are we from Copper Rocks?' Gloria asked. She tried not to look at the pony with its grim load.

'About two hours easy ride,' Luke replied. 'If you and Walt go ahead, I'll wait here for a few more minutes so we don't come into town together. That way the town busybodies won't bombard you with questions later. But you could warn the local lawman that I am coming. He might want to send out a wagon.'

'You sound like you might have brought in a body before,' Walt said lightly.

'I have. I used to be a Texas Ranger. But these days I'm sick of fighting Indians and outlaws and am looking for a ranch if I can find suitable land at the right price.'

'It does not look very suitable around here,' Gloria said as she looked at the barren landscape about her.

Luke thought quickly. 'You're right there,' he admitted. 'I'm going to see a rancher friend of my late father's. He has a spread north of here, somewhere along Duncan's Creek. He wrote saying that he knows of good country further north. I intend to have a look at it. Now, I suggest you folks start moving. I'll see you later in town.'

'When you get a ranch, will you also get a wife?' Gloria asked. 'Or do you have one already?'

'Not so far. I get into enough trouble on my own without getting into double harness.'

'So you're a confirmed bachelor?'

'Looks like it for a while,' Luke admitted.

The pair rode away. When they were out of earshot Walt turned to Gloria. 'Luke Adison is the man who was asking about Billy and the others in Yucca Springs. The bartender pointed him out to me. I wonder what he knows that we don't know? I'm not sure we should be letting him out of our sight.'

Gloria laughed. 'He won't disappear between here and Copper Rocks. We can stick close to him in town. I know the type. If I look helpless enough, he's sure to come to the aid of a damsel in distress. I think with a little effort I could talk him into joining our expedition. We can pretend that we know nothing about what he's really up to.'

'What if he shoots Billy on sight?'

'We will just have to make sure he doesn't.'

Luke resumed the journey at a steady walk. Normally he would travel a bit faster but he wanted the Hammonds to get a long start so that Gloria would be spared the commotion that usually accompanied the arrival of a gunshot victim in town. He wanted to meet them somewhere quiet and try to find out a bit more about their brother. The hunter should know the habits of his prey.

He rode slowly, deep in thought. Somehow he had to stay close to the Hammonds and hope that a careless word might provide a clue as to Billy's whereabouts. He doubted that the others would be in the vicinity just on the off-chance of finding their brother. They knew something. He was sure of that fact.

About a mile short of town a deputy sheriff was waiting with a two-horse team in a light wagon. He was a big, raw-boned man with a battered face that did not come from kissing babies. He introduced himself as Shadrach Payne and explained that a US marshal named Slattery was in town seeking the deserters. He wanted the body taken to a location where the townspeople would not see it. 'Seems like he wants to be sure who it is before folks find out about it. My boss, Sheriff Stone, can't see the need for such secrecy but has gone along with the idea,' the deputy said.

Slow of speech and deliberate in manner, Shadrach gave the impression that he was not the smartest but Luke saw the way his eyes darted about and missed nothing. He knew that the man was smarter than he pretended to be. Something about the way that his eyes flicked to the butt of Luke's gun and looked quickly away indicated that the deputy's curiosity had been aroused, though he pretended otherwise. It was time to lay a few cards on the table.

'I was wondering if you could help me.' Luke indicated the gun on his right hip. 'Have you ever seen anyone around here with a carved gun butt like this one? Mine is one of a pair. My brother Matt had the other one. He was a mail contractor who was robbed by his escort a couple of months ago and left to the Apaches.'

The deputy nodded. 'I heard about that — a bad business. I think too that I have seen a gun like that one of yours. Carved butts are common enough but that is beautiful work and it caught my eye as soon as I saw it. I know that I have seen a similar gun before but I didn't know the man who had it. It was just some stranger passing through.'

'Can you remember what he looked like?'

'No. He was kind of ordinary-looking,

40

nothing special about him.'

'Any idea how long ago you saw this *hombre*?'

'A couple of weeks, but I think it was after the time I heard about your brother. If I had known about that gun then I would sure have asked questions, but we've had US marshals and the army come through here and not one of them mentioned it.'

'Maybe they didn't know. I'll help you get our late friend aboard that wagon and then head for town. I've had enough travelling for today and I'm getting hungry.'

Together they loaded the dead man into the wagon and set out for Copper Rocks. When they got there Shadrach turned down a lane that ran behind the main street. Luke continued on his original course until he saw a livery stable and booked his animals into it. He saw the horses the Hammonds had ridden already settled into stalls with their noses deep in mangers. Leaving pack and saddles there, he slung his saddle-bags over his shoulder, took his carbine and crossed the street to the hotel. There was just time to book into a room, have a wash and a shave and don a clean but rumpled shirt that he had brought with him.

The dining room was dimly lit by several lamps and the smoke that came from them indicated that they were using poor-quality oil. It took a while to find the Hammonds but eventually Luke saw them at a table on the other side of the room. Unsure whether his company would intrude on their privacy, he selected a table some distance away.

The pair finished their meal and were leaving the dining room before Luke was halfway through the steak he had ordered. They paused briefly as they passed his table and Walt informed him that all had been reported to the sheriff and that the marshal would like to see him in the morning.

'Looks like tomorrow could be a busy day,' Luke said.

'Will you be in town for a while?' Gloria asked.

'I'm not sure. It all depends upon what tomorrow brings.'

Suddenly Luke decided to take a chance. 'I've heard there's a good view to be had from that hill just behind town. I was thinking of taking a stroll up there later. Would you folks be interested in coming?'

Walt laughed. 'I've had enough travelling for one day.' He turned to Gloria. 'You have always been keen on walking. Why don't you go? Luke can keep the rattlesnakes away from you.'

A look of concern came across the woman's face. 'Are there rattlesnakes up there? I don't want to go anywhere that those horrible things can be found.'

'They're all over this country and you have probably passed a dozen without knowing they were there,' Luke told her. 'I know what to look for and promise to keep you right away from any snakes.' He added, 'It's the two-legged snakes that are the most dangerous around here.'

Gloria thought for a while and then flashed a smile that absolutely entranced her would-be escort. 'Just give me a few minutes to get into some better walking-shoes. I'll see you in the lobby,' she called over her shoulder as she hurried away.

'I'll see you in the morning,' Walt said with a knowing smile.

Luke could scarcely believe his luck. Though he tried to tell himself that the outing was all part of his plan, he knew that he would enjoy the task he had set himself.

Gloria was quickly back and the pair walked slowly to the end of the town's main street where the road ceased and a footpath began. A rugged bluff of red and cream stone reared sharply before them for a height of about a hundred feet.

Luke glanced at the sun. 'I reckon we have about twenty minutes to sunset. After that we have about another twenty minutes before it gets too dark for walking. The walk to the top should only take us about ten minutes so we should really get a good look at the scenery before night falls.'

They took their time, occasionally stopping to admire the view or to allow Gloria to catch her breath.

'I didn't walk up many hills in New York,' she explained as she enthusiastically breathed in the fresh air. 'And there are so many people there that walking is not as enjoyable as this. Back East I would see more people in one day than a person in Copper Rocks would see in a year Have you ever seen a big city, Luke?'

'Not really, but I can't say that I really want to — specially not with all those people.'

'I can understand your reluctance. It's so peaceful out here.'

'Except when someone tries to shoot you,' Luke reminded.

They reached the top of the bluff and stood there watching the red-and-gold splendour of the setting sun. Luke was enjoying the company as much as the view, but now long, black shadows were creeping over the land and it was time to go.

Both seemed reluctant to start back but the rough track in darkness would be risky walking. As it was Luke found himself holding Gloria's elbow as they negotiated a few of the rougher spots. He found that he did not want to let her arm go and she did not seem to mind.

Too soon for his liking, they were back at the hotel and Luke reluctantly said good night.

'We'll have to do this more often,' Gloria said with a laugh as she hurried up the carpeted stairs to her room.

Luke stood a moment. Her perfume still hung in the air. Luke Adison, he said to himself, that's some girl.

5

Luke rose early and packed his belongings in case he needed to leave town quickly. He had finished his breakfast and left the hotel long before the Hammonds had arrived in the dining room. He would have liked to see Gloria again but forced himself to keep his mind on his real mission.

Sheriff Stone was doing his morning rounds but Marshal Thaddeus Slattery was reading a newspaper in the sheriff's office when Luke walked in. He was a thin man of medium build with a narrow, almost expressionless face and cold, blue eyes. There was no warmth in his handshake when Luke introduced himself and he was sparing with his words. 'Now, Mr Adison, suppose you tell me just what happened on the road there yesterday.'

With no need to worry about his role

in the affair, Luke did as the lawman requested. He saw both officers occasionally nod slightly in agreement when he gave his version of events.

Slattery listened impassively while the younger man gave his description of the shooting. Then he said, 'Your account agrees with what the Hammonds said. I can tell you now that you won't have any legal difficulties about that no-good deserter getting killed.'

'I'm a bit curious, Marshal, about the dead man's name.'

'His name was Fitzgibbon and you are right in thinking that he was one of the men who left your brother to the Apaches. But that is all I'm going to tell you except for a warning. Keep your nose out of this matter. There are some serious government investigations in progress and we don't want them jeopardized by strangers butting in. Is that quite clear?'

'It's quite clear,' Luke said as he left the office. He had no intention of complying with the lawman's directions but was being honest when he said that he fully understood them.

His next stop was the Territory Land Office. There was a fresh-faced young man behind the counter who smiled and asked Luke if he could help him.

'I hope you can. I have been offered a chance to buy some horses from a man by the name of Josh Coterill. The trouble is that I don't know where he is. I lost the letter giving me the directions. I know he has a place near Duncan's Creek but he said that the horses are kept miles away at another place he owns. I don't want to ride any further than I have to and was wondering whether you had a record of where the other place is?'

The man in the office did not hesitate. Things were quiet and he saw no reason why he should not help a member of the public even if the request was a little irregular. He opened a large, leather-bound book and turned over a series of alphabetically-marked pages. From the book, he transcribed a number on a piece of scrap paper, then went to a wooden filing-cabinet. After thumbing through a series of cardboard folders, he eventually selected one and opened it. He scribbled a few directions on the piece of paper and walked back to the counter. 'It's lucky you checked here first,' he told Luke. 'Joshua D. Coterill has one hundred and sixty acres on Barrel Creek, twenty-seven miles north of his other property on the road to Prescott.' He pointed to a large map on the office wall. 'You can see Barrel Creek to the right of the road. That quarter section would be just about where the creek does a bit of a dogleg and nearly comes up to the road. It should be easy to find.'

Carefully masking his excitement, Luke thanked the man and left. He knew now why government investigators had found nothing at Coterill's trading post. He felt sure that anything really incriminating would be hidden away at Barrel Creek.

He was returning to the hotel to

check out when he met the Hammonds outside a saddler's shop.

Gloria flashed him a friendly smile. 'You're just the man we wanted to see. Walt and I are going to buy a pack saddle and a horse to carry it. We can't stay in towns every night. It's too expensive and some towns are too far apart. Could you recommend something not too difficult for a couple of city folks to handle?'

'Packing is not a job you learn in five minutes. You need the right kind of saddle and need to balance the load properly. You also need the right kind of animal as well as being able to lash the packs securely. Why don't you hire someone to do your packing for you?'

'Would you like the job, Luke?'

He thought quickly. It would have its advantages. He tried to persuade himself that he would not really be taking the job for the pleasure of Gloria's company and that he might learn something new from the couple. But he needed to see what sort of

51

operation Coterill had at Barrel Creek. Reluctantly he said, 'I have another job to do first and could be away for a couple of days. If you are still here when I get back, I'll take the job. But if you're in a hurry, you should try to get someone from around here. The saddler or the livery stable operator should be able to point you in the right direction.'

Gloria looked disappointed. 'It would have been nice if we could have travelled together, Luke. There's a good chance we might not meet again.'

'I know that. But I hope we will. Why don't you and Walt rest here and see what you can find out over the next couple of days? I should be back by then.'

Later Gloria watched from the window of her hotel room as Luke rode out of town. She turned to Walt and said, 'I wonder what he knows that we don't?'

'Probably not much. We have the information that Billy gave us before he suddenly stopped writing. Luke knows nothing about Murdering Wells or he would have reacted when that dying man tried to tell us about it. It sounded like he was cursing someone.'

'That's an awful name for a place,' the girl said. 'I wonder how it got its name.'

Walt shrugged his shoulders. 'Who knows? One story is that the Apaches wiped out a party of Spanish explorers there once. Another story is that a crazy prospector murdered his two partners there. I'm not too concerned about how those wells were named but I am interested to know why Billy thought they were so important.'

'It's possible that that man's mind was already wandering when he talked that way or he might have been cursing you for shooting him. I wonder how much we should tell Luke if he decides to join us?' Gloria said.

'Let's worry about that if he decides to join us. My guess is that he will follow the same well-worn path to Coterill's trading post, strike a brick wall there and come back to see if we know any more than the rest of them. We should tell him just enough to keep him co-operating with us. If we don't need to mention Murdering Wells to him, we won't. If he does join us we will still need to be careful because he is the sort of hard customer who is likely to shoot Billy on sight. You might need to work on him and appeal to his better nature.'

'Leave him to me,' Gloria said, possibly a little too eagerly.

Walt looked at her suspiciously and continued, 'I was not expecting that fellow, Fitz, to turn up on his own the way he did. Do you think the whole group might have already split up?'

'They might have. Army pay is pretty poor. Billy has the money we sent him concealed in letters but the others could be like Fitz and have to start robbing people to make a living.'

Walt disagreed. 'I reckon the others would be trying to get clear of Arizona before drawing attention to themselves.

If what we heard is right, the army is patrolling all roads and even the back trails trying to stem the flow of deserters from this territory. Fitz was probably kicked out because he was unreliable and a danger to the rest of them. If Billy is even half as smart as he used to be, he will be lying low in some safe little hidey-hole until he can get clear of Arizona and the army.'

6

The man whom the army knew as Tom Pierce paced restlessly around in the small cabin. He was bored. He had been there too long and was eager to start his journey out of Arizona. Coterill had been vague about the length of time he would need to hide the deserters and the three men were sick of the little cabin hidden out in the brush.

Sandy Powell was seated on the cabin step whittling a stick. He was small with a youthful face currently set in an expression of utter boredom. Alan Hallam was playing solitaire with a dog-eared pack of cards that he was arranging on the rough table before the fireplace. He had added a beard to his large moustache and his hair was long and unkempt. Hallam had been a smart soldier but looked a very scruffy civilian.

'I'm getting sick of all this hanging

around,' Pierce complained. 'We've been hiding out here for damn near two months. I'm wondering whether Coterill intends keeping his side of the bargain and getting us over the border into Mexico.'

'From what we've heard, the law is all over Coterill and have turned his trading post inside out,' Hallam told him. 'He can't make a move until the fuss dies down.'

'If I could find those Murdering Wells, I'd be tempted to try getting across the Gila Desert without waiting for him,' Pierce growled.

Sandy looked up from his whittling. 'You won't find those wells on any map and you'd die in the desert. Some folks reckon they don't even exist and they're just a tale told by some loony old prospectors.'

'I'm pretty sure they exist or I wouldn't be cooling my heels here,' Pierce said. 'With the army and the law crawling all over the territory we can't get out by any of the usual routes.

Coterill's idea makes a lot of sense. We head out into the desert where nobody is likely to be and restock our water supply at the wells. Then we head south across the desert into Sonora. Coterill has a friend in a town there who will fit us out with false names and such and we can come back into the United States by way of any Texas border town. The law is looking for bad men leaving the country and won't be looking too closely at respectable folks coming back in.'

* * *

Luke left Copper Rocks early in the morning. Only a stray dog exploring the empty street saw him go. He was glad that the Hammonds were not with him. He could travel faster and would attract less attention alone. With Gloria Hammond he would certainly be noticed.

Two hours out from town he met a teamster heading for Copper Rocks. The man plodded beside the twelve oxen yoked to his wagon, his long whip dragging in the dirt behind him. He saw Luke but seemed in no mood for conversation, merely giving a grunt and a wave of acknowledgment as they passed. He was not the type who was prepared to impart information to strangers.

By noon the heat had increased and Luke was looking for a bit of water and some shade where his animals could rest for a while. Far ahead a dust cloud caught his eye, a high, thin cloud such as would be kicked up by ridden horses. Cattle and vehicles made heavier dust that stayed closer to the ground. He was more than a little worried because of occasional raids by Apaches and bandits and felt greatly relieved when he discerned men in blue uniforms riding in pairs toward him.

As the riders approached, he could see a man in civilian clothes riding beside the first soldier. The sunlight glinted on a silver badge pinned to his coat. Lawmen rarely travelled with the army so Luke knew that this was not a routine patrol.

When they met Luke greeted the sergeant-major at the head of the detachment and enquired about water ahead. The soldier pushed back a ragged black hat and rubbed his perspiring forehead, before replying, 'There's a little creek about two miles further on. You can get water enough for yourself and your animals there. It don't taste too good but it won't hurt you.'

'That's good. How far is it to the next store? I'm a little short of grub.'

The lawman, a thin-faced man with wrinkled features and, until then, an air of indifference, suddenly decided to join the conversation. He twisted in his saddle, pointed vaguely behind him and said, 'There's only Coterill's trading post, and then it's forty miles to Hansen Springs. You won't get anything at Coterill's except maybe some rotgut whiskey that he couldn't sell to the Indians. He don't welcome strangers unless he can short-change them in some sort of crooked deal.'

'Sounds like a good place to avoid,' Luke observed. 'I reckon old Lawyer will have to carry me another ten hours or so before we both get a proper feed.'

'Lawyer?' the sergeant-major said. 'Did you call him that because he was expensive?'

'No. He knows a lot of tricks to get people off. He's mighty sneaky and I keep telling myself I'm a fool to put up with him but when he's on his best behaviour not too many horses can stay with him.'

The lawman grunted. 'Wouldn't have a horse like that. Those sneak buckers always play their tricks at the most inconvenient times. A bullet in the head would do him the world of good.'

'There have been times when I reached the same conclusion but every so often this sneaky knothead surprises me by doing something extra good. I'm not sure whether he's a good horse with a touch of bad in him or a bad horse with a touch of good in him. We get folks like that sometimes but we don't go around shooting them until they prove what kind they are. Even then some never pay for their crimes.'

The lawman, in no mood for conversation with a person he saw as being no use to him, turned to the sergeant-major and grunted. 'Time we were moving. I want to be in Copper Rocks tonight.'

As he gathered up his reins, the soldier said, 'Don't be in too much of a hurry, Marshal. There's plenty of time and it ain't as if we have a lot to report.' Unawares, the man had answered the question that Luke had wanted to know.

He watched the riders file past him, bored, dusty men thinking mainly of their journey's end. He was almost certain that the patrol had just made another fruitless raid on the trading post. It would suit his plans if they had because it meant that the trader would not be quite as alert.

With a touch of the heel and a lift of his bridle hand, he called to the mule and started Lawyer back on their journey. When they reached the water, he slackened the cinches and allowed the animals to drink. The mule was reliable and would not attempt to roll in the shallow water with the pack as some animals did. Luke took a few strips of jerky from his saddle-bag, and chewed on the leathery dried meat until it became soft in his mouth. It was not the tastiest food he had eaten but was the most convenient for short halts on the trail. He made no effort to restrict the animals' drinking. They would be going back into steady work and would be thirsty again soon enough. During the short rest he considered a likely plan of action. He would avoid the trading post and hope that he could pass it unobserved. Then he would have to locate Coterill's Barrel Creek property and see what he could discover. The fear that he would find nothing was ever present in his mind even though he tried to discount that possibility.

About noon he passed a leaning post on the trail. It had a badly painted fingerboard attached, bearing the words TRADING POST and an arrow. A low-roofed adobe building and some corrals were situated about 200 yards from the trail in a clump of cottonwood trees. Two wagons were parked beside the house and Luke guessed that they were for sale but he saw no sign of anyone near the buildings.

Josh Coterill pressed his bearded face closer to the dusty window of his store. He cursed when he saw the rider on the road. After the raid by the law that morning he had tidied the premises and was now about to relax with his pipe and a bottle of whiskey. The last thing he wanted was a customer who would take up his time, look about and depart without buying.

Coterill was a man in his mid-forties, tall and broad-shouldered with long hair and a neatly trimmed black beard. He wore the usual working clothes of a man on the frontier except for an

Indian-made buckskin vest, fringed and ornamented with beadwork. He found that it added to his image as a frontiersman and enabled him to sell expensive and sometimes useless articles to unsuspecting greenhorns who seemed attracted to his premises. He wore no cartridge belt but the butt of a short-barrelled revolver protruded from his hip pocket.

Much to his relief, the stranger scarcely glanced in his direction and continued along the trail. But then instincts honed by years on the fringes of the law, took over. Something told him that the man on the road outside was no saddle tramp. It might have been the quality of his horse or even his apparent lack of curiosity, but the trader sensed that this man was different.

He sat in a chair from where he could see the trail and poured himself a drink. The tension caused by the morning's episode with the army was beginning to ease as the level of whiskey lowered in his glass, but the usual relaxed state did not come. The image of the passing rider kept coming to mind and his uneasiness grew.

Eventually he slammed down his glass and bellowed for his young assistant, who was working in a back room. 'Henry, get in here.'

7

The sun was getting low when Luke began to recognize the landmarks indicating that he was near Coterill's other holding. Little time had been wasted on the ride to Barrel Creek and his mount and pack were thirsty and eager to stop. He knew that the trader would not advertise any human presence and was not surprised to see what looked like a wall of pine trees that looked little different from other areas on the mountain slopes. But by looking above the tops of the trees at the red, rocky walls behind them he could see that they were growing across the mouth of a canyon.

No sign of any track was visible at first but Luke was sure that one would be there. He rode down a sloping bank to the creek and allowed his animals to drink while he looked about to see if they were being observed. Seeing nobody, he rode across the creek and through a screen of pine saplings. At a suitable place of concealment, he tied his animals to trees and proceeded on foot. It did not take him long to find a path that led deeper into the trees. Those using it had emerged at the creek in different places so that there was no worn track, but once out of sight of the road all had used the same path. It was a sure sign that whoever used the track had not wanted their presence to be noted.

A hundred yards into the trees Luke encountered a man-made barrier of pine logs that sealed off the entrance to a grassy canyon. A couple of poles were pulled across a narrow gap to form a gate and he saw the tracks of both men and horses on the bare trampled earth. He slipped through the rails following the path through a screen of trees and around a bend in the canyon.

The change was dramatic. The towering rocky walls opened out revealing a wide grassy flat upon which several horses were grazing. About 200 yards down the canyon he saw a small cabin and a corral. Worried that he might be seen from the cabin, Luke slipped back into the sheltering trees.

He could see about a dozen horses but four stood out. The 'American' horses, as Eastern-raised cavalry remounts were called, were easily identified by their size and uniformity of type. There were three bays and a sorrel, each a bit over fifteen hands in height and weighing around 1,000 pounds. The army paid big money for them and once they were acclimatized, they outlasted the mustang types common in the West. At the end of their army days some were sold to the civilian market, but they were well past their best and sales were subject to strict conditions.

Luke took advantage of every piece of cover and tried to stay out of sight from the cabin as he crept towards the nearest cavalry horse. A couple of mustang types grazing nearby raised their heads suspiciously and seemed about to move away, but the bay horse that he wanted to see was used to a lot of handling and took little notice of him. He could see that a bar had been branded recently through the US on the near shoulder, indicating an army reject, but the animal's legs appeared free of splints, scars or tendon damage and its feet were in good condition. In fact the horse showed little of the years of wear and tear that frontier cavalry remounts endured.

Taking a risk, Luke spoke quietly to the horse, walked up to it and caught it by the mane. It stood calmly while he peeled back the upper lip at the corner of its mouth. The first thing he saw was that the seven-year hook was still on the corner, upper, front tooth. This was no old animal worn out by service but one in the prime of life that the army ordinarily would not sell.

He knew then that he had found the horses ridden by the men who had abandoned his brother to the Apaches. But were the riders in the cabin? Luke slipped back under cover. He would watch the building for a while and see who emerged.

'I must be seeing things,' Sandy announced as he peered again through the burlap curtain that partly covered the glassless cabin window. 'I thought for a minute that I saw someone over near one of our horses. It might have been a trick of the shadows.'

Pierce jumped to his feet, alarm showing on his face. 'It could also be a lawman snooping around. Don't show yourself at the window but see if you can sight anyone hiding among the trees.' As he spoke Pierce picked up a nearby Spencer carbine and moved to where he could see out through the open door. Hallam peered around the edge of the burlap on the other window.

'I can't see anyone now,' Sandy told the others.

'That don't mean they're not there,' Pierce growled. 'We'll keep watch for a while and then, if we see nothing, you can go and have a look around. You look the most innocent among us just in case someone is curious. You know the story to tell.'

The baby-faced deserter did not seem too perturbed. 'I'm not even sure I saw anyone there. Maybe I'm getting jumpy from being here too long.'

'It don't hurt to be careful,' Hallam declared, his face a mask of concentration as he studied the scene from his window. 'I wish those horses were closer. For all we know the law could just be waiting for us to come and get them.'

'Horses won't help us if the law's out there,' Pierce muttered. 'This canyon only has one way out. It's a good hideout but once it's found it becomes a trap. The sooner we're out of here, the happier I'll be.'

Luke was safely among the trees when he glanced back and saw a man emerge from the cabin door. He was small and wiry with sandy-coloured hair and appeared unconcerned as he walked casually among the horses. He spoke softly to a lean pinto pony and extended his hand. The pony eyed him suspiciously for a moment, then stretched out its neck and snatched the piece of biscuit that was offered. To an observer he was just someone getting on better terms with a horse but, while his actions appeared totally innocent, he looked more relaxed than he felt. Sandy stroked the pony's head and spoke softly to it as he casually scrutinized the landscape.

That's probably Billy Hammond, Luke told himself. He bore little resemblance to a hardened criminal. The young man wore no gun and, petting the horse as he did, was the picture of innocence. For the first time the concealed watcher could understand his sister's claim that he might have been forced into deserting. There was no point in waiting longer. He knew that the others would be there. Now he could plan his revenge. Keeping well under cover, he crept back to where he had left his animals.

He was back on the trail to Copper Rocks when he saw a young man on a sweaty sorrel pony come galloping towards him. The newcomer wore no gun and hardly acknowledged his presence, just gave a quick nod of the head as he urged his horse past.

Someone in a hell of a hurry, Luke told himself.

Sandy had barely returned to the cabin when he heard the beat of galloping hoofs. Hallam heard them too and grabbed a carbine as he hurried to a window.

Pierce also armed himself but then relaxed when he saw the approaching rider. 'It's Henry. Looks like he has some news for us.'

The boy reined in before the house and wasted no time on greetings. 'Do you know the rider who was just here?' he demanded.

'We didn't see any rider.' Pierce replied. 'What's happening?'

'A rider with a packmule passed the trading post today. Coterill sent me to see what he was up to. I just passed him going back the way he came. His tracks showed that he'd been in here, probably spying on you.'

'So I really did see someone.' Sandy sounded pleased. 'I thought I must have been seeing things.'

'Too bad you weren't.' Hallam did not share his relief.

'The law's on to us,' Pierce said. 'We have to get out of here. The only other way is to catch up with that *hombre*, on the road and shoot him.'

'He has a long start by now. We mightn't catch him,' Sandy argued.

Henry looked pleased with himself. 'There's another way. Give me one of those mustangs out there. I know a short cut back to the trading post. It's rough but will take miles off the trip. If I go now, I reckon I can get ahead of that snooper and me and Coterill can set up an ambush along the trail.'

'Are you sure you can do it?' Pierce did not sound convinced.

'Short of the pony killing itself

somehow, I know I can beat that lawman back to the trading post. I can go over a lot of places that the road has to go around. But it's my guess that our man will camp the night somewhere along Barrel Creek or even over the hills on the upper reaches of Duncan's Creek, so I should have plenty of time.'

'Supposing something goes wrong.' Hallam still had serious doubts. 'We're caught here like rats in a trap. If we have to go alone, how would we get to Murdering Wells?'

Henry turned to Sandy. 'Catch that black mustang for me and put my saddle on it while I explain the way to Murdering Wells.'

Pierce was suddenly suspicious. 'It's supposed to be a secret. How do you know?'

'It ain't all that secret. A few old-timers know about it and I've been there myself. An old Papago Indian took me out there once on a hunting trip. Coterill pretends it's a great secret but the wells are easy to find with the right directions.'

Turning to Sandy, Pierce ordered, 'Get that horse pronto for our friend here. We don't want to delay him too long. While he's doing that, Henry, you can give me a few directions.'

A cunning look came into the boy's eyes. 'Josh don't like other folks knowin' the way to the wells. It's his special secret. He seems to think that other folks don't know but there's a few around this area who have been out to Murdering Wells. How much will you pay me for a map?'

Pierce thought quickly. He suspected that Henry was not used to having large sums of money. 'How about ten dollars?'

To Henry ten dollars was a fortune. If Pierce was happy to pay all that money for a secret that wasn't really a secret, he was happy to oblige. 'Get me a pencil and some paper. You just bought yourself a map.'

'Are you sure you can give us the

right directions?'

Henry nodded confidently. 'You can bet your life on it.'

'I know I will be, but your life is on the line if it's not right.'

8

Luke was elated by what he had discovered but before taking his revenge, he had to be sure that he had correctly identified his targets. He had nothing against deserters as such. They were a fact of life with the poorly paid, overworked frontier soldiers, but those who had deserted Matt to the Apaches were, to his mind, devoid of any human decency.

He decided that he was not going to the law. They had not been helpful. But he would try to make some arrangement with the Hammonds. They seemed decent people and by pointing out their brother, could positively identify the group. He was prepared to do a deal with them, even to the extent of letting their brother go free if he stayed out of the shooting. That was something he would negotiate later. The kid looked harmless enough.

Night had fallen but eventually he found a grassy spot where he could camp for the night. His animals could rest and feed there after their long day's work. He unsaddled Lawyer and the mule and watched them roll in a patch of dust as he prepared his camp. Then he hobbled them and staked them out with long ropes connected to the centre rings of the hobbles. The other ends of the ropes were attached to a couple of cavalry-style picket pins driven into the ground. This arrangement allowed the animals to graze about in restricted areas while being close enough to reach quickly if necessary.

After a quick meal he rolled out groundsheet and blankets in a spot where he would not be easily seen and settled down to sleep.

Mules had an inbuilt suspicion of the human race and Luke's was as good as any watchdog. It would alert its owner to any intruders long before they found where he was sleeping. He would sleep lightly because as far as Luke was concerned, he was in enemy territory.

★ ★ ★

Coterill did not appreciate being woken by Henry's frantic hammering on his bedroom door but he restrained his anger. His young assistant was well trained and knew better than to wake his boss over trivial matters.

'What do you want?' the trader bellowed.

'There's trouble, boss. That stranger you had me follow went straight to Barrel Creek as though he knew where to look. Them soldier fellas spotted him near the cabin. He was lookin' for somethin'.'

'Where is he now?' Coterill climbed into his pants and boots as he spoke.

'He's headed this way. I saw his tracks then took a short cut to make sure I got here ahead of him. Chances are that he'll stop and camp but if he don't he could be here in half an hour or so.'

'We have to stop him getting past here. I'll take a rifle and stake out the spot where Duncan's Creek crosses the trail just north of here. I want you to get Dave Robbins. Tell him there's fifty dollars in it for him if he feels like joining us. I know he will. He's always broke. Bring him to the creek crossing as quick as you can. Now get going.'

Robbins was Coterill's closest neighbour, a poor man who was always happy to earn a dishonest dollar. It suited the trader to have a willing henchman living nearby. He made a point of throwing a bit of work his neighbour's way just to stop him abandoning the quarter-section on which he had homesteaded. Suitably bad company was not always easy to find.

'I'm awful hungry, boss. Is there anything to eat?'

'Not much time for that, Henry. There's some biscuits in the kitchen and a bottle of whiskey under the counter in the store. Have a snort of that and chew the biscuits as you go. If that *hombre* gets past us, we're in hell's own trouble.'

★ ★ ★

The morning star was showing when Luke arose. He had slept well and felt refreshed. The large circular areas of chewed-off grass around each picket pin showed that the horse and mule had eaten well, and they had been well rested. His breakfast of cold sardines and biscuits would not have appealed to many. It was convenient though, and a drink of strong, black coffee quickly washed away the taste of the canned fish that otherwise would have lingered in his mouth during what could be a long, dry ride.

It did not take Luke long to pack up his gear and secure it on the mule. Lawyer humped his back a little when saddled. He was in one of his tricky moods and his near eye rolled back as the rider prepared to mount. Luke shortened the nearside rein and growled at him, letting the horse know that he was in no mood for rambunctious behaviour. It had been a while since he last tested his rider. 'If you try any of your tricks this morning, Lawyer, I'll rip your goddamned ears off.'

The horse knew by the tone of his rider's voice that he meant business and postponed any plans for an excessively energetic start to the day. The sun was just showing as a red line on the eastern horizon and the daytime birds were awakening as Luke took the trail again.

Coterill had taken a position over-looking the creek crossing and guarded it until Henry and Robbins arrived two hours later. By then, being both cold and tired, he was not in the best of moods. He ordered his neighbour to keep watch and stretched out behind a log in order to catch up on a bit more sleep.

Henry, who was the most tired of all, soon followed his boss's lead and within minutes was sound asleep on the hard ground.

Robbins made himself as comfortable as he could on a flat-topped boulder that allowed him a good view of the trail. His rifle was a long infantry, breech-loader in .50/70 calibre, a souvenir of his days as a buffalo hunter. At close range the big lead bullets it fired had a devastating effect but to be doubly sure its owner was in the habit of scoring the tips of the bullets with a knife to ensure that they expanded even further or even broke up on impact.

Confident that he was as ready as he could be, Robbins produced a pipe and proceeded to ream out the bowl with a pocket knife. When satisfied with his efforts, he filled it with tobacco and lit it. Only then did he return to his task of watching the trail. He scarcely noticed the approaching rider in the faint early morning light and Luke was a mere hundred yards away before Robbins noticed him.

He rapidly exhaled the smoke he had drawn in and jumped down from his perch. 'Josh,' he whispered urgently. 'Someone's coming.'

'What's up?' Coterill demanded, still half-asleep.

'Shhh — that *hombre* you're after is coming down the trail.'

Given the poor light and distance, Luke was not aware of the men ahead but Lawyer was. He had smelled the pipe and faintly heard the voices.

Luke felt the animal tense its muscles and it started blowing nervously through its nostrils. He followed its gaze but saw nothing at the side of the trail ahead. 'Don't get playing any of your tricks on me this morning,' he growled at the horse. 'I ain't in the — '

A man's head and a long rifle barrel suddenly appeared over a rock a short distance down the trail.

Its worst fears confirmed the horse shied violently, throwing Luke slightly off balance. Few rogue horses can resist the urge to unseat an unbalanced rider and the buckskin was no exception. He launched himself into the air and dropped his right shoulder on landing.

The rifle boomed at the exact moment that Luke was spilled from his saddle.

9

He hit the ground hard but Luke hardly felt the pain. His big concern was the man with the rifle. Lawyer's gyrations had caused the shooter to miss but the range was such that he was unlikely to miss twice.

As the riderless horse bucked away, the mule followed it and ran between its owner and Robbins. This slight delay was enough for Luke to draw his Colt and roll into a shallow ditch beside the trail. The cloud of gun smoke gave him a rough indication of the shooter's position and he was lining his sights on the top of the boulder as the man with the rifle reappeared. He was squarely in Luke's sights when his intended victim squeezed the trigger.

Henry jumped in alarm as Robbins fell back against him before collapsing on the ground. Given more time to think, the boy might not have acted as he did but, surprised and half-dazed from lack of sleep, he ran around the boulder behind which the dead man had been sheltering. He had a rifle ready to fire but first had to locate his target. He had not seen Luke thrown from his horse and had only a general idea of where he was likely to be.

Luke had the advantage of seeing his target first and fired a shot as carefully aimed as circumstances permitted. The bullet took Henry in the upper arm, knocking the rifle from his grasp and throwing him back behind the boulder. Shocked but still full of fight, Henry raised himself to a sitting position and awkwardly reached for his revolver with his left hand. But then the pain from his shattered arm hit him and he swayed and fell back.

Coterill had seen enough. His two assistants had ceased to be a force with two shots. Robbins was dead and the amount of blood pouring from the severed artery in Henry's upper arm was a clear indication that he would soon be likewise. The trader had no intention of joining the casualty list.

'Keep him busy, Henry,' he whispered. 'I'll try to get around the side of him.'

If Henry heard him it was unlikely that he understood, because he had already slipped into a semi-conscious state. But Coterill had no intention of carrying on the fight. He crawled away as silently as he could until he knew that he was out of sight of the road. Then he ran as quickly as his lack of condition would allow, half a mile through the brush to his trading post.

Luke remained crouched in the ditch expecting another gunman but knew that he could not stay long in case someone was creeping through the brush seeking a place to outflank him. The little ditch only gave minimal protection from a frontal attack. There was a bank of earth behind him and a heavy growth of mature pine trees that offered more protection while allowing a better view over the ambush site. Chancing a bullet in the back, he jumped to his feet, ran up the sloping bank and threw himself behind the trunk of the nearest big tree. Much to his relief, no shots followed him. More confidently, he darted from tree to tree until he was in a position to look down on his would-be killers. When higher up the ridge, he could see the body of Robbins in the untidy sprawl that was characteristic of a dead man. It was a while before he located Henry. A pair of legs, partly obscured by rocks and bushes, showed where his second attacker was situated. The legs were stretched out with the toes of the boots pointing upwards, indicating that their owner was in a sitting position looking towards the trail. Luke knew that Henry was wounded but he did not know how badly and a determined wounded man was still capable of firing a fatal shot. Because of this, he spent half an hour creeping through the brush before he reached a position where he could see, from the amount of blood, that his victim had bled to death. As far as he knew there had only been two attackers so he holstered his gun and walked down to see what he could learn from the dead men.

He recognized Henry as the young man he had seen the day before, but he found no identification on him. Robbins was a stranger and Luke could see that he was lucky that the shooter had a single-shot rifle. The slight delay in reloading had given him time to draw his own gun and seek cover. Any suspicion that the two were merely bandits was soon dispelled when he realized that no horses were hidden nearby. He knew that Henry must have possessed a horse to get in front of him. He distinctly remembered seeing a sorrel pony. Where was it?

Though he was not sure of the exact distance, Luke knew that he was somewhere near the trading post. But first he had to find Lawyer. Satisfied that he could glean little useful information from the pockets of the two dead men, he set out in the direction that the animals took. The long, trailing reins had hampered Lawyer but he was smart enough to hold his head to one side avoiding stepping on them until he found a suitable patch of grass. He had discovered good grazing just around the bend in the trail and the mule was with him. Luke counted himself lucky that he had not needed to walk far. 'You miserable son of a mongrel-bred coyote,' he said to the horse as he picked up the reins. 'You nearly got me killed. I ought to give you a bit of a going over with the spurs and see if you enjoy bucking when I'm ready for you.' But then he realized that being thrown when he had been, had probably saved his life. His bruised hip was aching from where he had rolled on his gun, so he tried to maintain his anger but weakened. 'Just don't do that again,' he said sternly as he swung into the saddle. 'Now let's go and see what Coterill knows about all this.'

Coterill knew immediately that his little criminal empire was in ruins but recent pressure from the law had forced him to consider such an eventuality. In the brush on the hill behind his home he had concealed an escape kit in a pair of saddle-bags. There was jerky, ship's biscuit, some canned food and $1,500 in notes. A large canteen full of water was also there in case he had to hide in dry country for a while.

When he arrived back at the trading post Coterill wasted no time. He stuffed his remaining spare money in one pocket of his coat and a box of rifle ammunition in the other. Then, with his Winchester under his arm, he locked the back door of the post from the inside, left the building and secured the front door with a large, strong padlock.

Expecting to see Luke coming at any moment, he caught his tall, roan horse and saddled it. With a feeling of relief, he climbed into his saddle and rode off into the brush. His provisions were cached in a place that afforded a good view of the trading post from behind a screen of young pines. He was just fastening the last of his supplies behind the cantle of the saddle when he saw the distant figure of his pursuer turn from the trail and ride towards the trading post.

Luke was sure that Coterill was behind the failed ambush and was uncertain as to the reception that awaited him at the trading post. Fifty yards short of his objective, he dismounted at a small grove of cottonwoods and tied Lawyer there. Then, rifle in hand, he advanced in a series of short runs trying to keep at angles that would make life difficult for a shooter inside the building. He quickly saw the external lock on the front door but suspected it could have been a trap to make the building appear empty. Keeping clear of the windows as much as possible, he worked his way to the back of the building. There was only one small window, which he could easily avoid, but the back door was a strong one that had been locked with a key.

'Anyone home?' he shouted. No reply.

The temptation to force an entry was strong but Luke was pretty sure that he would find nothing incriminating and if Coterill was lurking nearby, it would give him an excuse to shoot a suspected burglar. After raids by US marshals, the trader would be unlikely to leave any vital evidence at his home so there was little point in Luke delaying. Reluctantly he retraced his steps to his horse. There were a few horses in a small pasture beside the trading post and one showed the marks of saddle and cinch in dried, white sweat on its black hide. He guessed then how the boy with a fresh horse and better knowledge of the country, had managed to get ahead of him to arrange the ambush.

Coterill, safely hidden on the hill watched his hunter ride away. He felt a degree of satisfaction that his foresight had paid off and had few regrets about leaving his business. It had served its purpose and he had enough money to start again somewhere else if he could get clear of Arizona. A short spell in Mexico appealed to him just then but the only way to get there undetected would be by way of Murdering Wells. He resolved to pick up the deserters on the way, not through any loyalty to them but because they could be damning witnesses against him if captured.

Coterill guessed that he would have at least a full day before Luke brought any law back from Copper Rocks. Without a backward glance at the place he was leaving, he climbed aboard the roan and pointed its head towards the hidden cabin on Barrel Creek.

10

Luke reached Copper Rocks in mid-afternoon and halted before the sheriff's office. This time Sheriff Morgan Stone was present. He was a big, powerful man in his late thirties with a face that showed evidence of more than one violent disagreement with recalcitrant customers. Shadrach was busily sweeping out the cell area but looked through the connecting door and nodded as he saw the visitor.

Introductions were brief. Stone listened in silence as Luke recounted the day's events. His bushy eyebrows nearly met in a frown as the account ended. Then he said suspiciously, 'What is there about you that seems to attract road agents? You came in with a dead one just the other day. And what were you doing up at Duncan's Creek in the first place?'

'I was looking at land,' Luke told him. In a very general sort of a way that was the truth but he changed the subject quickly. 'That road agent who got shot the other day was after those Hammond people, not me. And, if you recall, Walter Hammond shot him as well. If you had been there you would not have thought twice about ventilating his hide either. The bore of a Spencer rifle looks awful big when it's pointed straight at you.'

'What did you do with the bodies? Shadrach and I will go up there tomorrow and collect them.'

'I covered them with brush and heavy branches to keep scavengers away. All their personal effects are with them. They are in the rocks on the right side of the trail about fifty yards north of where Duncan's Creek crosses the trail, maybe half a mile from the trading post. There was nobody home when I called there this morning. I stacked a few rocks in a cairn on the right side of the road so you can see where the bodies are.'

Stone looked at him suspiciously. 'Why is it that you can't guide us back?'

'I hurt my hip when my horse unloaded me during the ambush. I might need to rest up tomorrow.'

'I'll expect to see you here when we get back. I reckon there'll be a few questions to answer.'

'I'll be happy to answer any questions you have about this shooting, Sheriff.' Luke spoke the truth there but did not specify just when he would be answering any questions. His immediate plans did not involve the lawman.

★　★　★

Gloria Hammond knocked on Walter's door in the hotel. He opened it quickly and let her in.

'Luke's back in town,' she said quietly. 'I saw that yellow horse of his outside the sheriff's office. It might be time to find out how much he knows.'

Walter looked worried. 'He wasn't

gone long. Probably found as little as the law did.'

'I'm not so sure,' Gloria said. 'If he found nothing, why would he be seeing the sheriff? I think it's time we had a little talk with our man from Texas. If he intends staying he'll have to put his horse in the livery stable. I can see it from my room. As soon as I see him going that way, I'll go down there to check on our horses. I'll ask him to help us arrange a pack animal. It will be an excuse to get him talking.'

'Unless you have lost your touch,' Walter chuckled, 'you won't have any trouble getting his mind off horses and mules.'

★ ★ ★

Coterill rode hard, pushing his mount to the limits of its endurance. It would last long enough to reach the Barrel Creek hideout where he would find a replacement and after that he would abandon the animal. It was almost sundown when he turned along the hidden trail to the cabin.

He had dismounted at the rails in the front fence when Hallam stepped from behind a tree with a carbine in his hands.

'I damn near shot you, Coterill. You're lucky I decided to take a good look at you first. Did you get that snooper who was here?'

'No. There's a heap of trouble coming. Put the rails up after me and then come back to the cabin. We could soon have the law on our heels. That stranger killed my two men and he's sure to run for the law at Copper Rocks.'

When the trader had flogged his weary pony up to the cabin door, Pierce hurried out to meet him. The anxiety clearly evident in Coterill's face told him that the rider had not brought good news.

'What's gone wrong, Josh?'

'This place has been discovered. That's what's wrong.'

'So you couldn't stop that snooper,'

Pierce said in an accusing tone.

'Two men died trying and you could have stopped him yourself if you had kept a proper lookout,' the trader replied angrily.

Sandy intervened then. 'How long do you think we have before the law gets here?'

'Less than a day. I want you to take those army horses and every piece of military equipment you have and hide out in the broken country over the mountain behind this place. There's grass and water in the coulees there. Make sure you leave no trace of your presence here. I'll stay around so that when the law arrives, all they'll find will be me on my own property where I have a legal right to be.'

'What if we make for Murdering Wells?' Sandy asked.

'It's too soon. You need to hang around here for at least another week.'

'Why?' Hallam demanded. He was still panting from hurrying back to the cabin.

Coterill was quickly losing his patience. 'There's a lot of reasons and I don't have time to explain. Trust me. Now get moving.'

Hallam might have argued but Pierce, who was standing behind the trader, signalled him to be quiet.

For the next couple of hours all worked frantically to remove evidence of their stay in the cabin.

* * *

The two Hammonds contrived to meet Luke at the livery stable when he went to feed and rest his horse.

'Just the man I was after,' Walt said heartily as they entered the stable and saw him unsaddling Lawyer. 'Sis and I were just coming down to make sure that our horses were well. Have you thought about our offer?'

Luke looked around. The stable hand was working nearby tidying a row of empty stalls. 'Later,' he whispered to Hammond. 'I have news for you.'

Gloria's blue eyes missed little and she observed, 'You're limping, Luke. Have you been hurt?'

'Not really,' came the reply. 'My horse got out from under me this morning and I rolled on my gun after I hit the ground. It's sore but nothing serious.'

Gloria laughed. 'It doesn't look like anywhere a lady could kiss and make better.'

'That doggone horse does nothing right,' Luke said in mock anger. He turned to the horse and demanded, 'Why didn't you throw me on my face, you knothead?'

The Hammonds laughed and kept up a flow of small talk while the stableman was in earshot. Then they walked outside.

Safely away from curious listeners, Luke announced, 'I reckon I've found your brother.'

'Is he well?' asked Gloria.

'He looks fine. He's in some mighty bad company, though. I'm sure he was one of the escort that deserted my brother.'

'What are you going to do about it if you find that he is?' Walter asked nervously.

The smile also disappeared from Gloria's face.

Luke thought for a while. 'If you could really identify your brother, I'll try to take him alive. I might not be so careful with the others. But if he fires one shot in my direction, I'll shoot back.'

'But if you capture Billy and hand him over to the law, the others might incriminate him,' Walter pointed out.

'They can't if they're dead,' Luke said quietly.

'Billy's not a criminal,' Gloria insisted. 'We know that he must have been forced into this. Does he have to be turned over to the law?'

'I'll make a deal with you. I'm going after those men in the morning but I have to notify the law all the same. With any luck I'll have a couple of hours' start on them. If you two are ready to ride with me at 5 a.m. we can leave a note under the sheriff's door. He's going as far as Duncan's Creek and can follow us up later. That will give us a few extra hours. If you can identify your brother I'll try to get him away from the other two. If I succeed, and he gives the right answers, you can take him and run but I intend handing out a bit of long-overdue justice to the others. Nobody has to know that you were with me. Is that a deal?'

Walter looked worried and scratched his chin before turning to his sister. 'There are a lot of ifs and buts in that arrangement but it might be the best deal we get. What do you think?'

Gloria did not hesitate. 'It could be the answer to our prayers. I doubt we will get a better deal. I agree to it. I know we can trust you, Luke.'

'So do I,' Walter agreed. 'What do we need to do now?'

Luke explained his plan. 'We travel light. Just one blanket apiece and some easily carried food in our saddle-bags, nothing that needs cooking. I will leave my packmule here until I get back. Make sure you have a water canteen each but don't fill it. Water's heavy and there are places ahead where we can fill the canteens if we have to. What do you have in the way of guns? I don't want to get you involved in any shooting but things are mighty unpredictable.'

'I have a .38 revolver and today I bought a Winchester repeater,' Walt told him.

'Let's hope you don't have to use them.'

Gloria was keen to show that she too could be relied upon in a fight. 'I bought a Whitney .32,' she volunteered. 'I'm a good shot. I used to practise with a saloon pistol back in New York.'

Luke was not impressed. 'Those saloon pistols have very little powder in their cartridges so they are safe to use indoors. You might find that the .32 shoots a little differently. If any shooting starts, don't get involved. Leave that to

Walter and myself.'

They did not linger long at the stable after making arrangements to collect their horses early. The Hammonds paid their bill but Luke said that he would be back. They all settled their hotel accounts and prepared for the next day's journey.

Luke wrote a note advising the sheriff of what he had found and said that he was going ahead to keep watch on the deserters. Deliberately he did not mention the Hammonds or state the number of men who, he suspected, were hiding at Barrel Creek. If he was to release Billy Hammond, it was best that only his family knew of his presence.

11

It was still dark when the three met again after what had been a very short night's sleep. They said little as they hurried to the darkened stable, which by previous arrangement had been left unlocked for them.

With years of practice, Luke had his mount ready to go while the two Hammonds were still fastening their equipment. He told them, 'It might be best if I go now so that no one will see us leaving together. I'll wait for you along the trail.'

'Sounds like a good idea,' Walter said. Then he remembered. 'Have you written that note for Sheriff Stone?'

'I have.'

'Give it to me and I'll put it under the door. The sheriff's office is in the opposite direction to where we want to go, so if Gloria and I go there first, any early risers will think we went in that direction. That way, even if someone sees us later heading the other way, it won't look as though we are travelling with you.'

'Good idea,' Luke agreed as he handed over the note in its sealed envelope.

It was nearly two hours later before the Hammonds caught up with him. He had found a good patch of grass and was giving Lawyer a rest and some grazing time while he waited. The horse was a good one but he had covered many miles over the last few days and his owner wanted to spare him as much as possible.

When the others caught up, Luke set a fairly solid pace where the terrain permitted. The others were used to travelling much more slowly but did not complain, because they were aware that time was precious.

The sun was still low in the eastern sky as they passed Coterill's trading post. They allowed the horses to drink where Duncan's Creek crossed the road but Luke thought it best not to mention the two dead men concealed nearby. He was hoping that the deserters were not early risers as he estimated that at least two hours' travelling time still lay ahead of them.

Gloria was looking tired. Already she had ridden further than she would normally ride in a day but she made no complaint. Neither did Walter. He looked far from comfortable but knew that time was important.

'This would be a nice ride,' Gloria told Luke, 'if we had time to slow down and enjoy the scenery.'

'Let's hope you have that time soon and that you and Walter will be able to enjoy it with your other brother.'

'It would be nice if you could be with us, Luke. What do you intend to do when all this is over?'

'I hadn't given it much thought — maybe go back to Texas.'

'Are you sure there isn't a girl there?'

Luke shook his head. 'I've never

spent enough time in the one place to get to know any girls. If I find a little spread of my own somewhere I might try to find someone to settle down with. But I doubt that I would ever be a very attractive marriage proposition and not every girl wants to live on an isolated ranch somewhere.'

'You might be surprised. Walter and I like what we have seen of the West. New York is too busy and crowded. We were only talking last night about buying a ranch out here somewhere but we know little about horses and nothing at all about raising cattle.'

'If you hire a couple of hands who know what they're doing, they could help you get started.'

'Would you be interested in helping us to get set up if we found a suitable place?'

That prospect appealed to Luke greatly but he felt that he should be realistic. 'That would be good but you would need to get well away from here and your brother Billy will need to be further away still. The law has a long memory.'

'Once we get Billy out of this scrape,' Gloria said sternly, 'he will be on his own. We want to give him a new start in life but after that, it is up to him to make something of himself.'

'We have to get him out of the scrape first, Sis.' Walter reminded her. Then he said to Luke, 'Give our offer some serious consideration, Luke. We seem to be able to work well together. We could put up the money and you could supply the necessary skills.'

'First things first, Walter. We have to try to get Billy clear of that gang without causing a ruckus and that won't be easy. If things go wrong, you and Gloria could finish up hating me for ever.'

The girl smiled sweetly. 'I'm sure that would never happen.'

'I wish I was so sure,' Luke said fervently.

They halted for a while on a ridge that gave them a good all-round view.

The Hammonds were glad to stop and dismounted stiffly as they tried to loosen aching joints. Luke took a small canvas bag from his saddle-bag and opened it. 'Time for something to eat,' he announced. He opened the bag and held it for Gloria. 'Help yourself — it's jerky.'

The girl extracted a hard piece of dried, brown material that looked like a cross between wood and leather. Her nose wrinkled as she regarded the jerky with distrust. 'Are you sure this is safe to eat?'

'It hasn't killed me yet. Just bite a piece off and it will soften in your mouth. When it gets soft, you chew it. I suggest that you eat something now because we are not far from that cabin and it might be a while before you get the chance to eat again.'

Walter walked across and took a strip of jerky. 'Where is the hideout we're going to?'

Luke pointed to a distant ridge crowned with juniper trees. 'There's a shack behind that ridge just in front of that mountain with all those trees on it. That creek coming around the end of the ridge is Barrel Creek. Our men are there somewhere if they haven't already high-tailed it.'

Gloria sounded disappointed. 'Do you think they could be gone?'

'I would if I was one of them, but people are unpredictable and they could be a bit slow getting away. We should know in about half an hour. From here on we ride on the right side of the trail where there are a few trees to give us cover. They might have a lookout on the next ridge so we will need to be careful.'

They resumed their journey riding in single file. Luke rode about twenty yards ahead of Walter with Gloria following behind. He hoped that if the deserters had left a sentry he would see him before being spotted. But he need not have worried. The trio reached the top of the ridge with no alarm being raised. Though a logical spot to post a sentry, there was no sign of one.

They did not linger on the crest of the ridge where they might be seen on the skyline but descended to a point where they could see the water of Barrel Creek flashing silver amid the dark green shade of the surrounding pines. About a hundred yards from the bottom of the hill Luke found the place he sought. Tall pines, jumbled boulders and undergrowth combined to make a good hiding place. He guided his companions in there and dismounted.

'Wait here for me,' he instructed. 'The cabin is not far away on the other side of the creek but you can't see it from here. I'll go forward on foot and have a look around. I could be an hour or so. If you hear shooting, get on your horses and get going. Don't wait for me.'

'We wouldn't run out on you, Luke,' Gloria protested.

'Don't argue. If trouble starts my chances are better if I only have myself to look after.'

116

'He's right, Sis,' Walter said quietly. 'We could be in the way trying to fight experienced Westerners in this sort of country.'

'Those horses need minding,' Luke told them. 'It's important that someone holds them. We can't afford to lose them, so it's not as if I am making you people simply spectators. I'll see you in an hour or maybe sooner.'

★ ★ ★

Coterill and the deserters had slept later than they intended and now the soldiers were scurrying about saddling horses and carefully removing any traces of their presence.

Sandy had fewer possessions than the others and quickly had his horse saddled and ready. Pierce ordered him to ride to the gate and act as a guard while the others made their final preparations. Though no longer in the army, the young man was still in the habit of following orders and Pierce, a dominant

117

personality, had assumed the leadership role for the group.

While it was originally decided that the deserters should leave their American horses and use mustangs, the former could prove an embarrassment to the trader, so he wanted them out of the way. Provided he was not arrested, the horses could be swapped again before the journey to Murdering Wells and Mexico. With all trace of the deserters gone and no American horses, the trader was confident that he could bluff his way through any questions the lawmen might ask. He could plead ignorance of the failed ambush and claim that he was at Barrel Creek when it occurred.

Sandy's former troop horse was fat and full of energy after weeks of good grazing and it snorted and spooked at a variety of imaginary dangers as he rode it to the rails that closed the hidden pasture. It also disliked being away from the others and moved about restlessly when its rider dismounted.

The deserter hoped that the noise the animal was making would not betray his position but drew some comfort from the thought that a posse could not be expected for some hours yet. He thought that Pierce was being over-cautious but was happy to be away from the frantic activity at the hideout. From his position he would have a good view of the path that led straight to where he waited while bushes screened him from anyone approaching. He left his carbine on his saddle, being reluctant to load it unless absolutely necessary. The Spencer had justly earned its 'fool killer' reputation and careless handling had led to cartridges exploding in the magazine. Sandy saw no need to load it because he had no intention of becoming involved in a gunfight with any intruders. He would fire his revolver to warn the others, jump on his horse and flee back to the hideout.

He would not have been so relaxed had he known that he was already being stalked.

Luke knew where the gate to the hideout was situated and rightly assumed that a guard could be posted there. He waded through the creek at a point well away from where the regular crossing was, then quietly stole through the undergrowth and trees. His progress was slow because silent movement was difficult. He was only too aware that any careless move or accidental noise could betray him, with fatal results.

He heard the horse trampling about and snorting impatiently some distance before he could see it through the trees, so he knew that there was a sentry. Now his caution doubled. He had to see the other man before he himself was seen.

Through a break in the shrubbery he saw a flash of colour that he recognized as part of a faded red shirt. The sentry was barely ten yards away. For a few seconds Luke studied what he could see of the man. The rails and some bushes were between them but he could see the upper part of the sentry's body. It was the sandy-haired young man he had seen before, the one he guessed was Billy Hammond. This was a stroke of unexpected luck. If he could get him back to his brother and sister, he would have the other deserters nicely trapped. Part of him said that his vengeance would not be complete until all four deserters were dead but for the sake of Gloria Hammond, he was prepared to spare her brother. He was almost willing to believe that Billy had been forced into doing what he did. Vengeance suddenly seemed less important than winning Gloria's heart.

The immediate problem was how to capture the sentry before he could resist and possibly warn the others. The horse sensed his presence but because of its previous activity, the boy seemed unaware of the danger. He spoke softly to the horse and continued looking towards the creek crossing.

Luke stole closer. Now only a couple of yards separated him from his man but, try as he might, he could find no way of silently crossing the intervening ground. There was another doubt too. What if the sentry decided to go for a gun? He doubted that the woman would forgive him shooting a member of her family. He guessed that Walter would have similar strong family feelings or he would not be where he was. The Hammonds were a complication he did not need, but Luke told himself that he was stuck with them.

He had reached the conclusion that there was no way he could move closer to his intended victim so Luke knew that he had to take a calculated risk. Much could go wrong but he hoped that it would not.

Carefully he drew his gun and cocked it as he stepped from cover. 'Hold still, and no noise,' he said softly. 'I don't want to kill you but I will if I have to.'

The sandy haired one went pale with shock but retained his senses enough to slowly raise his hands.

12

'Not a word out of you. Just do as I say and you'll get a pleasant surprise.' But the menacing tone of Luke's voice left his prisoner convinced that he was being sarcastic.

'Who are you?'

'You'll find out later. Now hand me your gun, lead that horse out through the rails and don't say another word.'

With great trepidation Sandy followed instructions. Leading his prisoner's horse Luke forced him to wade across the creek to a clump of young pines beside the trail.

Every cavalryman carried a thirty foot lariat attached to his saddle in a tightly wound hank. Luke ordered his prisoner to lie on the ground while he detached the rope and expertly hogtied him. Then he used Sandy's bandanna as a gag. 'Now just lie there quietly and someone will be along shortly to release you. This is your lucky day.'

The prisoner made a few muffled sounds but Luke took no notice of his protests. He mounted the horse and rode it back up the trail to where the Hammonds were waiting.

'I reckon I've got your brother,' he said as he dismounted.

Gloria's face lit up and she flashed a happy smile. 'That's wonderful.' Then she looked puzzled.

It was Walter who asked the question. 'Where is he?'

Luke explained. 'He's tied up in a clump of young pine trees on the right-hand side of the trail at the foot of this hill. I have to take my own horse and get back to settle matters with the rest of them. They might have already missed Billy so I have to be quick. Untie him, get him on his horse and get him out of here. The sheriff's posse might not be far away, so go quickly. If it's not your brother, leave him tied up.'

'Will we see you again?' Gloria asked.

'We don't want to lose track of you now,' Walt added.

'I don't know for sure but you could send me a letter if you get clear of this mess. The post office in Boulder Creek, Texas, will know where to find me if I get back in one piece.'

Walter grabbed Luke's hand and shook it. 'We can't thank you enough, Luke.'

Gloria threw her arms around him and planted a large kiss on his cheek. At another time he would have been tempted to linger but now time was precious. Reluctantly Luke disentangled himself and mounted his horse. 'I have to go. Good luck folks.'

Not far away, Pierce and the others were ready to move. Coterill had scattered his belongings around the cabin to make it appear that he had been in residence there for a while. He disliked letting the stolen cavalry horses go but had no choice as they could now incriminate him. He knew though, that the deserters would swap them back for mustangs when the law had left the area. He still had control over the others as they needed him to guide them to Murdering Wells.

But there was one deal that he still wanted to make. From the moment he saw it, he had coveted the ivory-handled gun that Pierce was wearing and he knew that it was not military property. 'Would you consider doing a deal on that gun?' he asked.

'What are you offering?'

'Twenty dollars, hard cash.'

Pierce laughed as he swung aboard his horse. 'Forget it, Josh. When we get to Mexico some grandee will give me nearly twice that for this gun.'

'That's too bad. You can't go to Mexico for a couple of weeks yet. You have to stay around here. I'll tell you when it's safe to go. Hide out here on the mountain and when you see me sending up chimney smoke at midday, you'll know when it's safe to come back. Then I'll guide you to Murdering Wells and it will be plain sailing all the way to Mexico.'

'Why do we need to stay around here?' Pierce growled. He liked to be in control of situations that so directly concerned him.

The trader had his reasons but resented having his decisions queried. Instead he said harshly, 'I'm running this operation and know what has to be done. Right now I have more important things to do than stand here answering questions. You'll just have to trust me. I know what I'm doing and have damn good reasons for waiting.'

Though he secretly differed, Pierce made no reply to the trader. He signalled to Hallam who was leading the army horse that Fitz had ridden and the pair turned their mounts away toward the creek. 'We'll pick up Sandy as we go,' he told the other deserter.

Still angry that his planning had been questioned, Coterill watched them cross the open meadow and disappear into the trees. He suspected Pierce of intended treachery but was unsure of the form it would take. Previous experience with dangerous men had taught him the signs to look for and he was sure that at present he was dealing with one. Pierce worried him more than the impending visit from the government officers.

Luke had returned to the trails and was riding quietly through them when he caught a glimpse of movement through the trees ahead. He grabbed his Winchester and swiftly came out of his saddle. No sooner had his feet hit the ground than two men with three horses appeared through the pines only a short distance away.

'Get your hands up!' Luke gave the command out of force of habit even though he knew it would not be obeyed.

Hallam immediately went for his gun and received a well-aimed rifle bullet as a consequence. Even as the stricken man rolled from his saddle, Luke was seeking his next target. Unfortunately though, Hallam's horse turned across between him and Pierce in its panicked efforts to escape. Forced to jump back to avoid being trampled, Luke could not get a shot at the second man before he wheeled his horse back into the trees. Pausing only long enough to ensure that Hallam was dead, Luke followed on foot. He knew that the cabin was not far away. He reached the edge of the trees in time to see Pierce dismounting before the building.

The rifle seemed to jump to Luke's shoulder of its own accord as he saw his target heading for cover. He saw too, a flash of an ivory gun butt protruding from the man's holster, so he squeezed the trigger without hesitation, but Pierce's luck held. His horse, turned loose, wheeled away in alarm and turned right into the bullet intended for its former rider. Hit in the brain, the animal crashed to the ground, almost falling on Pierce as he dived through the cabin door.

Luke tried a bullet through the door, hoping to hit the man as he closed it, but a rifle boomed from the cabin window and a near miss buzzed past his ear. When another bullet kicked up the dirt at his feet he retreated a couple of yards to take cover behind the trunk of an ancient pine tree. A slug smacking solidly into the tree trunk told him that the men in the cabin had seen where he was sheltering. Another bullet blew a section of bark off the side of the tree, so Luke dropped to the ground where a couple of large roots gave him added protection as he peered from cover.

His enemies made no attempt to emerge from their shelter, but he figured that the cabin would have a back door, or at least a window, so they would not necessarily come after him through the front door.

The inside of the building was thick with gunsmoke but Coterill and Pierce were in no hurry to leave it.

'How many are there?' the trader asked as he peered cautiously around the edge of a window.

'Only one as far as I know, but he got

the drop on us and Hallam didn't last a second.'

Coterill thought for a while. A one-man posse seemed most unlikely. Then he remembered the stranger they had failed to ambush. 'Did you see a buckskin horse?'

'Yes. Do you think it is the stranger you saw yesterday?'

'I'm damn sure it is but I don't know what game he's playing. Could he be after you?'

'I ain't got any enemies except Uncle Sam. You would have made more enemies around these parts than I would have.'

Coterill fired another shot at Luke's position before growling, 'That coyote out there could have a posse coming behind. If he has, how am I going to explain your presence and that dead army horse that's across the doorway? I know that the brands have been altered and I have a stolen army authorization book to cover the sales, but those papers are strictly for civilian benefit.

The army knows the officers authorized to dispose of cast horses and will soon check out the signatures. We're in one hell of a mess here and our friend behind the tree is covering the only way we can get out with horses.'

'Is there any way one of us could slip out by the back door and get around behind him?'

'One of us could get out through the back door,' Coterill said, 'and creep round through the brush to where a side-on shot at him would be possible. That way we'd have him in a crossfire.'

Pierce looked coldly at the trader. 'A good idea. You know this place better than me — what are you waiting for?'

Coterill was about to object but something in Pierce's manner told him that it would be a waste of breath. 'Just make sure you keep him busy,' he said sullenly. 'Remember, I'm the only one who knows the secret of how to get to Murdering Wells.'

Though his face betrayed no emotion, Pierce thought of the map that

Henry had drawn. I have news for you, he thought as the trader left by the back door.

Luke guessed that the front door would not be the only way out from the cabin and decided to seek a better position. He reasoned that if he could get around to the end of the building, he could cover both front and back and, if there were no windows in the end, his enemies could not see him. There was cover to his left and he could work his way through the brush to reach a commanding position. The movement would attract a shot or two but he knew that the army, to cut costs, gave recruits very little firing practice with live ammunition. With the element of surprise he was fairly confident of reaching his new position unscathed.

Suddenly jumping from behind the tree, he sprinted to a boulder partly screened by a blackberry bush. The bullet that Pierce fired went nowhere close to him. Then, crawling on hands and knees, Luke was able to keep out of sight and move to an angle that would make it difficult for his enemies to shoot at him from the small cabin window. Somebody inside fired another shot but the blindly fired bullet came nowhere near his present position. It was a waste of lead and for a moment he thought that the deserters were starting to panic, but then the thought came to him that the shot might be meant as a diversion. When another bullet was sent into the brush in a similarly haphazard manner, Luke was sure that it was part of a plan to keep him occupied.

The uneasy feeling that someone else was stalking him through the brush crept into his mind. Aware that sudden movement attracted attention, he turned his head slowly to the left. He had a clear view on the right side, so the danger would come from the opposite direction.

But before a man began to stalk him he needed to know where his quarry was and Luke resolved not to make that task too easy. He crouched low in the chaparral with rifle thrust forward, moving only his eyes. It seemed ages before he heard stealthy footsteps in the brush. He listened. The sound told him that there was only one man. The next noise was easily recognizable. It was leaves brushing off clothing and it was very close.

The gunman in the cabin fired again but Luke took no notice. The person approaching was close enough to be heard panting slightly with the unexpected exertion of walking around a relatively steep section of hillside. Then Coterill stepped out of the bushes and found himself staring down the muzzle of Luke's rifle.

Reason disappeared and reflexes took over. Coterill went to raise his rifle, cocking the hammer as he did so. The shock was showing on his face long before the bullet from Luke's rifle hit him in the mid-section. The impact threw the trader backwards and he rolled down the slope he had just ascended. As soon as he stopped rolling though, the trader, who had retained his hold on his rifle, fired back. The shot was a hasty one that went wide of its intended mark. With painful slowness, the wounded man worked the trigger guard of his Spencer carbine to reload for another shot. Luke took no chances and sent another slug into the man who was trying to raise his weapon again. As the second bullet tore into him, the rifle fell from Coterill's hand almost as if he had suddenly lost interest in what was happening to him. His hands clawed furrows in the soft grass, then he fell back, staring with lifeless eyes at the man who had killed him.

One glance at the Indian beading on the dead man's vest told Luke that he had just accounted for the trading post proprietor. He had not been specifically after Coterill but the trader had thrown in his lot with the wrong side, so Luke was not unduly troubled. One more deserter remained and that man was probably wearing his brother's gun.

He slipped another couple of cartridges

through the Winchester's loading port and moved to a position where he could see the building end on. No openings faced him so he knew that the man inside would have to emerge from one of the doors to even see where he was.

Pierce had heard the shots and, as the distinctive sound of the Winchester came last, he correctly assumed that Coterill was out of the fight. Frantic now, he peered through the windows but could see nothing. He dared not open a door in case the unknown gunman was standing there. It would be suicide to go outside, so Pierce resolved to stay where he was in the hope that the stranger would try to enter the building where the man inside would have the advantage.

Luke worked his way towards the end of the cabin. He was in the open but was sure that the last of his enemies was safely penned in from where he could not escape.

He was striding toward the cabin's front door when something hit him in the calf of the leg and knocked him over. He heard the gunshots then and another bullet buried itself in the ground beside him. He rolled to the partial shelter of a small rock, then darkness closed in on him.

13

'He's coming round.' A familiar voice brought Luke back to consciousness. His head was aching, his face was stiff with dried blood and there was a burning pain in his right calf. Then he became aware of Walter, Sandy and Gloria looking down at him. Both men were pointing guns at him.

'What's happening?' Luke mumbled. His mind had not really grasped what had occurred.

An unfamiliar voice snarled, 'You're about to get killed. That's what's happening.'

Still not fully aware of the situation, the wounded man painfully turned his head. He saw a stranger, a man who had his brother's gun on his hip and an angry expression on his face. 'You weren't as smart as you thought you were, you badge-toting sonofabitch.'

Luke was still having trouble understanding what had happened. He looked at Gloria. 'What are you doing here?'

The girl laughed harshly. 'You captured the wrong man. My fictional brother is the one you were trying to kill. Actually we are not related but are linked by the same business.' She continued: 'Sandy here decided to throw in with us. It was his shooting that hit you. You have a bullet through your leg and were hit on the head by a ricochet off that rock there, or possibly a piece of the rock. You're lucky you have a hard head.'

'For all the good that will do you,' Walter added ominously. 'You're no use to us now, Luke. You helped us find Billy but now you present a major problem. Hard luck, but we have to part company.'

The one thing that Luke understood clearly was that he was in dire peril and needed to keep talking. 'You're digging yourself and your sister into a lot of trouble. Aren't you forgetting the letter I sent to Sheriff Stone?'

Walter produced the envelope from an inside pocket. 'Oh dear.' He chuckled in pretended concern. 'I forgot to deliver it. Now nobody knows where we went or what has happened here.'

'That's where you're wrong. There's always somebody who saw something. The law will be coming up this way whether you like it or not because of the two dead bodies I left beside the trail near the trading post. Most towns these days are linked to the electric telegraph. No horse can outrun that and the army is watching the roads for deserters. Coterill might have known some back trail that would get you clear of the state but he's dead now.'

Pierce interrupted at this point. 'We don't need Coterill. I have a map showing how to find Murdering Wells. They are old Indian wells in a desert where most folks think there is no water. From there it's an easy ride to Mexico.'

'You'll need more than a map,' Luke told him. 'If you miss those wells you'll the in the desert. There won't be any bucket and windlass to show where they are. Indian wells are often just small holes in the ground that they sometimes cover with a rock to stop evaporation. You could ride right past it and never see one.'

The looks on his captors' faces told Luke that he had sown the first seeds of doubt among the group. It was a start, but to stay alive he would need to build on their misgivings.

Pierce turned to Sandy. 'You've been in the cavalry longer than I have. Have you seen an Indian well?'

'Never have. I came in the draft of reinforcements ahead of yours. I'm originally from Vermont where every-thing is different from here. There's a heap of water there. It's nice and green, not desolate like this country.'

Luke had found a weakness. Now he had to exploit it. 'I think we could do a deal here. It could work out well for all concerned. What if I guide you to the wells and you leave me there to find my own way back? You'll be in Mexico long before I get back to civilization.'

Walter was looking worried. Both he and Gloria had found travelling with horses difficult and they had been in reasonably settled areas. Neither felt confident of their ability to travel in featureless desert. Pierce and Sandy were frowning too. They had seen just enough cavalry service to leave them in awe of those who could find their way about in such country. Neither was confident that he possessed the necessary skill.

'I don't need help from you.' Pierce was talking as though trying to convince himself. 'You're just trying to save your hide.'

'Of course I am. I'd be a fool not to. But I can tell you this: without me you don't have much chance of finding that water even with a map. I know how to recognize Indian wells. They are often hidden on purpose. You'll most likely all die in the desert if you are just going by a map.'

Gloria spoke then. The sweet, gentle lady who had charmed Luke was now replaced by someone coldly practical. 'You're shot. You might not be able to travel anywhere.'

'I'm sure my leg isn't broken. I think the bullet went straight through the calf. Give me a chance to clean it up and patch it a bit and I should be able to ride. It will hurt but it's a lot better than being dead. And for sure, much as I would like to, I won't be able to run away from you. You sure had me fooled, Gloria. It looks like I fell for the oldest trick in the book.'

'You certainly did.' Walter chuckled. 'Gloria's not my sister. She's my wife.'

'That's your problem.' With those sharp words, Luke closed the subject and tried to cover his disappointment and sense of betrayal. Survival now was more important than one treacherous woman. He took a risk and decided to force the issue with the group's leader.

'Are you interested in my offer, or not?'

Pierce exchanged glances with his companions. All nodded in agreement. They were aware that it would be a simple matter to dispose of their prisoner after he had served his purpose.

'Is it a deal?' Luke prompted.

Pierce hesitated for a moment and then said, 'It's a deal but if you make one wrong move, you're dead and we'll take our chances without you. That's the only warning I'm giving you.'

'That's fine by me. Now if you will let me get up, I'll try to find something in that cabin to try to patch up this leg.

Sandy leaned down and took his arm but in his free hand he held the revolver that Luke had been carrying. 'Don't do anything stupid,' he warned, 'or you'll get shot with your own gun. I figure I'm entitled to it because I'm the one that stopped your little tricks.'

Luke made no comment as he struggled to regain his upright stance and put some weight on the injured leg.

When he did, it hurt but the wounded limb took his weight. Awkwardly he limped to the cabin. He knew that walking and riding would be painful, but to survive he had to remain mobile.

Trying to conceal his pain, he hobbled to the cabin with Sandy keeping a close eye on him. Inside he found a clean shirt that Coterill had left. He ripped it into bandages while some water heated in a can over the fire that he had started in the fireplace. Under Sandy's watchful gaze he found a jar of salt in a wooden box on a shelf. He threw a handful of salt into the water and screwed the lid back on the jar. 'It might be a good idea to take this with us,' he told his captor. 'We might have to live on game, and any sort of meat without salt gets monotonous pretty quickly.'

Sandy looked doubtful for a moment, but then took the salt out to add to the supplies they were packing on to a spare horse.

Luke was bathing his wounded leg

with the salt water when Pierce came into the cabin. He looked at the wounded man and demanded, 'How long are you going to be? Don't try delaying us. Get a move on or I'll shoot you and take my chances in the desert without you.'

Though he knew that the deserter meant every word, Luke outwardly ignored the threat. 'Are you sure you have all you need for a desert journey? For instance, do you have a bucket? You might need something to get water up if the well is a deep one. Chances are you'll need ropes to lower the bucket, too.'

'We have ropes and can lower canteens into the well. We don't need no buckets.'

Luke disagreed. 'You're wrong there. Have you ever tried to water a thirsty horse from a canteen? The other horses would be fighting to get at the water long before the first one had a drink. You would spill more than the horse got.'

Pierce needed no more convincing. He suddenly saw that Luke was a useful asset to their party and was picking up details that they had completely overlooked. 'Get that leg patched up quick, then see if there's anything else lying about that we forgot. I saw a bucket outside. We can take that.'

It took Luke another twenty minutes to clean and bandage his wound and wipe some of the blood off his face. The head injury had bled a lot but was not serious. By this time Sandy had returned and as Luke adjusted the bandage around his leg, he asked, 'If you aren't the Hammonds' brother, who is?'

The young man laughed. 'They fooled you completely. There wasn't any brother. Like the Hammonds told you, they ain't brother and sister. It was just an act to make people less suspicious of them. They're married but reckon that the law back East could be looking for a married couple. They fooled you into thinking they were

148

looking for a black sheep brother out of family loyalty. From what I was told, Pierce was a safe-cracker in New York. He stole a lot of cash from a bank vault that he blew but the law was on his trail. He hid out by joining the army under another name and got clear of the city by going west with a bunch of recruits. Trouble was that he then had to get clear of the army. We had heard about Coterill's business trading with deserters, so Pierce wrote to the Hammonds for a bit of extra help. They had always been part of his old gang and are keen to help him spend the money he stole. The opportunity to desert came up before the Hammonds could get out here and we had to take it. That's why they had trouble finding us. I know, because of your gun, that you are some kin of the mail contractor we left in the desert. We didn't know there were Apaches about. It was just bad luck.'

Luke was about to make an angry reply but thought better of it. Sandy was inclined to talk and he needed all the information he could get if he wanted to stay alive. His ignorance of the true situation had greatly contributed to his peril so he knew that he must learn all he could about his enemies and exploit any weaknesses he found.

Another surprise awaited Luke when he eventually hobbled outside. Pierce was mounted on Lawyer. 'I reckoned it would be safer if I took this good horse,' the deserter told him. 'He looks like he could outrun any of these others and we would not want you leaving us out in the desert.'

Luke saw no obligation to warn Pierce about the horse's nasty habit of bucking. It was something that later he might be able to turn to his advantage. Instead he limped over to the weedy little mustang that had been selected for him. Because of his wounded leg, he had to find a piece of uneven ground and mount from the high side. The procedure was painful though and he guessed that he would find little comfort on the long ride ahead.

Pierce rode over to Luke with a piece of paper in his hands. 'According to these directions we go north to the headwaters of Barrel Creek. Do you know where Barrel Creek is?'

'This creek we're on is Barrel Creek.' Luke pointed up into the hills as he spoke. 'We just follow the creek until it runs out. That's easy enough. Where do we go from there?'

'I'll tell you when we get there,' Pierce growled. He saw no reason to trust his new guide and was not giving away any unnecessary information.

They started along the creek bank with Pierce leading and Luke riding behind him. Sandy and Walt would make sure that he did not escape.

'It will be easier for the horses if we keep the creek in sight without going too close to it,' he told Pierce. 'These mountain creeks tend to get deep narrow beds and a lot of brush along the banks. We'll make better time if we work higher on the slope and just keep the creek in sight.'

Though offering no comment, the leader turned his mount further up the hillside. He's taking notice, Luke told himself as he wondered how to turn the situation to his own advantage. Two could play at the art of deception but first he would be helpful. His very survival depended upon winning a certain degree of trust.

For the next hour the horses struggled up a hillside that gradually became steeper. The animals were sweating freely and the ground beneath their hoofs was crumbling, sending rocks bouncing down into the valley below. The creek had gradually become smaller and was now merely a trickle. They were still below the crest of the range when Pierce pointed ahead to a cluster of boulders. 'Where's the creek? There's no sign of it on the other side of those rocks.'

'It's a spring,' Luke explained. 'The creek starts here. This is your first landmark. Where do we go from here?'

Pierce consulted his notes. 'We ride south-west for about three hours and we should strike a dry creek bed.'

'Where do we go then?'

'I'll tell you when we get there,' Pierce said, making no attempt to conceal the distrust in his voice. 'Now turn south-west.'

Luke turned his horse toward the crest of the range. He could see another possible flaw in Pierce's planning but it would be better to exploit that later.

'Are you sure you're heading the right way?' Pierce demanded suspiciously.

The slope was dotted with barrel cactus plants and these lean in a south-westerly direction, so Luke was sure of his course, but he saw no reason to pass this information on to his captors. 'I know where I'm going,' he said quietly.

The scene from the mountain top was a daunting one. Red desert dotted with clumps of cactus and mesquite stretched away into the heat haze. The country was mostly flat but the occasional mesa stood like a stone monument above the plain.

After one glance at the arid landscape ahead Luke turned to Pierce. 'We should have watered the horses and filled our canteens back at the creek because it looks mighty dry out there. It's crazy to go into that country without water.'

The suggestion that they had to return to the water did nothing to improve Pierce's temper. He swore and snarled, 'You picked a fine time to tell me about that. It means covering extra distance and we're losing time by going back.'

Luke reminded him. 'You were the one who was giving the directions. I'm not a mind-reader. The desert is a risky place to travel. You had better start trusting me with a bit more information because I don't want to die out there any more than you do. Now, let's get back to that water. We can't waste time and later have to be looking for landmarks in the dark.'

It was nearly an hour before they returned to the mountain top but humans and horses had all drunk deeply and all canteens were full. The horses slipped and slid on the steep descent and Luke was forced to put more weight on his wounded leg. He could only grit his teeth against the pain and hope that the exertion did not reopen the two holes that the bullet had made. He was worried too about infection and knew that blood poisoning could easily develop. A wound that was minor in a town with medical help could prove fatal out in the desert.

14

Luke had ignored the Hammonds as much as he could. Their treachery had angered him and he felt foolish that Gloria had tricked him so easily. They rode at the rear with Walt leading the packhorse, and gradually the distance increased between them and the others.

The riders were far out on the flats when Luke looked back and saw the couple a good hundred yards behind. In his present mood he was tempted to let the inevitable happen but, for some reason, had second thoughts.

'We're going to lose the Hammonds,' he called to Pierce. 'They're getting too far back and sure as hell will lose sight of us and take a wrong turn when we get into that high brush I can see ahead.'

'They can follow our tracks,' Pierce replied. He was worried by the arid landscape and would not relax until they reached the wells.

'Dudes never look down. They think that only Indians can follow tracks. I don't care if we lose them after the way they double-crossed me but that pack-horse could be mighty useful.'

The deserter swore under his breath as he halted Lawyer and looked back. 'Sandy,' he ordered, 'go back there and hustle them along. Tell Gloria to come up here and you stay there making sure that Walt keeps up. We can't afford to be separated in country like this.'

Luke smiled to himself. 'My horse likes to walk at the back,' was the traditional dude's excuse for dawdling and he did not doubt that Sandy would soon be hearing it.

A short time later Gloria trotted past, her cheeks flushed with annoyance and placed her mount beside Pierce's.

'I don't have to take orders from you,' Luke heard her complain.

'If you want to keep living you do.'

Luke noted the discord and wondered

how he might turn it to his advantage. He glanced at the sun and guessed it was nearly three hours since they had left the water. He wondered too about Lawyer. He was sure that the horse would attempt to throw his rider at some stage and wanted to stay close enough to take any opportunity that offered. But the horse was totally unpredictable.

A cluster of ironwood trees attracted Luke's attention. Trees usually grew along watercourses even if the latter were mostly dry. 'Looks like a bit of shade over there,' he called. 'We'll need to rest the horses and have a bite to eat, so this could be as good a place as we are likely to get.'

The deserter argued against stopping at first. He was keen to make as much distance as possible while the horses were relatively fresh. However he saw reason when his prisoner pointed out the folly of taking too much out of the horses on the first day.

They found the dry creek bed where Luke guessed it would be and even found a spot in the shade where they could escape the worst of the sun while they rested. Their meal was hardly sumptuous, a swallow of water, some stale, hard-to-chew biscuits and the last of Luke's jerky. The dry food was hard to swallow but they were hoarding their water. Only Pierce knew how far it was to Murdering Wells and he was not saying.

Luke's leg was getting sorer and he wondered uneasily how much longer he would be able to keep travelling. If he was to get out of his predicament he would need to act quickly. Pierce would shoot him or abandon him in the desert if he failed to keep up with the party. He had seated himself on the creek bank so that it would be easier to get to his feet. The Hammonds were nearby but he ignored them, speaking only to Pierce.

'You have our second landmark. Now where do we go from here?'

The deserter consulted his notes. 'We have to ride south along this creek bed for another three hours or so until we see an ironwood tree about a hundred yards away on the bank to our right. Do you know what an ironwood tree looks like?'

'I know,' Luke said shortly. He thought it best not to tell Pierce that the same trees were affording the shade in which they had halted. The more his captors had to depend upon him, the safer he was.

It was time to create a bit more confusion. 'Those directions you have are mighty vague. Depending on horses and riders, an hour's ride could be anywhere between three and five miles. We could be looking at nine miles or fifteen miles. There's one hell of a difference.'

Luke guessed that the journey would probably be about ten miles at the pace most people travelled in the desert. The pace of five miles per hour actually involved a fair bit of trotting and cantering but he saw no need to tell his captors this. The more he worried them the better he liked it. He could see that Pierce was uneasy as he ordered the party to continue.

Climbing back into the saddle was painful for Luke and his leg had stiffened during the rest. It would be a long, uncomfortable ride. Another doubt nagged him, too. Only Pierce would know when they were nearing the wells and Luke knew that his usefulness to the others would end when they reached the water. If he was to escape he would soon need to do so. He was not bound but wounded and mounted on an inferior horse; flight was out of the question. Somehow he had to get his hands on a gun. Quickly assessing the strengths of his captors, he thought that his best chance of obtaining a weapon lay with the Hammonds.

Gloria was riding ahead with Pierce, so Luke slowed his horse until Walt and Sandy caught up with him. 'This danged horse is feeling the heat,' he said by way of explanation.

'How much further do we need to go

today?' Walt asked.

'You'd better ask Billy or Pierce or whatever he calls himself. He's the only one who really knows where we're going and sure as hell, he's keeping it a secret. It's a bit of a worry being steered by a greenhorn in this country. He might not know he's lost till it's too late.'

'Don't worry about Pierce,' Sandy said. 'He's smart. He wasn't long in the cavalry but he learned mighty quick. The officers thought he was just great. That's why he was put on the mail detail. He was already acting corporal.'

'That may be,' Luke growled. 'But only he knows where we are going. If he leaves us or if anything happens to him, the rest of us could die out here. I wouldn't trust him an inch.'

'You don't have to. You're on the other side,' Sandy reminded him.

'Until we get out of this desert, we'd best all be on the same side. Getting to Murdering Wells is only halfway to safety.'

Sandy was not worried. 'From what we was told, it's only a day's ride south from the wells to Sonora.'

'I think you'll find it's a mighty long day and if you strike a sandstorm you won't know what direction you're heading.'

Walt looked at the clear blue sky. 'There's no sign of any storm up there.' He smiled. 'You wouldn't be trying to worry us, would you, Luke?'

'I'm only worrying about my own hide.' Luke had seen enough. Hammond's gun was in a shoulder holster under his waistcoat. It would be easy for its owner to reach but hard for anyone else to snatch.

Sandy was his next option. He was young and alert but had unwittingly made his gun easier for someone else to grab. He was wearing it butt-forward for a cross draw. Many law enforcement officers disliked this arrangement because anyone facing them had a good chance of grabbing their holstered weapon. Luke knew that Sandy offered the best chance of obtaining a weapon. Now he had to choose the right time to make his move. While Walt and Sandy rode together any attempt to grab a gun was unlikely to succeed. The pair seemed to have developed a friendship and for most of the journey had ridden together at the rear of the group.

Gloria and Pierce seemed to be getting on well together and occasionally those at the rear heard her laugh. Walt glowered and though jealousy was showing on his face, he said nothing.

Luke made a mental note to exploit that emotion if the opportunity arose. At present he knew he had little to gain so it would be a case of biding his time.

All were hot and thirsty when Luke sighted the ironweed tree that was their next landmark. 'There's your tree, Pierce. Where do we go from here?'

'Are you sure it's the right tree?'

'I'm sure. There's not a lot of them around and that one is where your instructions say it should be. I can't steer us any more if I don't know which direction we're supposed to be going. Sure as hell there's no well around here.'

Almost grudgingly the deserter told him, 'We go straight west from here to the top of that ridge over there and look south-west.'

'Then we'd better get a move on. The sun will only be up for another hour or so and we can't travel in the dark.'

The group moved on and after travelling a short distance they passed the skeletal remains of a horse. Such sights were not uncommon but Luke noted one aspect that the others did not. The dead horse's head was pointed back the way they had come. Chances were that the animal, in its death throes, could have fallen with its head in any direction but something about the sight made Luke feel uneasy. He said nothing to his companions.

At the crest of the ridge, Pierce halted and looked to the south-west. Many miles away, across a sun-scorched plain, a tall rocky column stood alone, a very obvious landmark.

'That's our next marker,' Pierce said as he pointed. 'Let's go.'

'We won't make it tonight,' Luke told him. 'That spire of rocks is much further away than it looks. It's easy to underestimate distance when you have a clear view over open country. It would be night before we got there and could miss it in the dark.'

'So what? We'd see it in the morning. But if we ride faster we might still get there before night falls.'

Luke shook his head. 'It would take too much out of the horses. For all I know they could be facing a day without water tomorrow. We have to nurse those horses right to the wells. It's time to stop keeping secrets, Pierce. How far from the wells are we?'

The deserter relented. 'We should reach the water tomorrow. That's all I'm telling you. I'll take your advice, though, about stopping. See if you can find a place where we can camp for the night. We need to make an early start in the morning before the sun gets too hot.'

They descended to the plain and Luke found a place where fallen branches from a few long-dead trees would provide them with firewood, while the trunks would serve to anchor the picket line. They could not afford to lose their horses. His leg was very painful and it was an effort even to unsaddle his horse. As he went to put his saddle down, he lost his balance and fell over.

Gloria was closest and to Luke's surprise she hurried over to assist him. 'Are you all right?' she asked anxiously.

'Why the sudden concern?' There was a harsh note in his voice.

She said softly, 'I know you have little reason to trust me but I had to go along with the others. We are all in great danger here. There is something going to happen soon. That's all I can say. Can I count on you to help me when the time comes?'

'Get me a gun and I might consider

it but at present I can't even help myself. I fell for your story before, Gloria, so I'm a bit wary of anything you tell me now. I didn't hear you shouting any warnings when Sandy tried to kill me.'

'I can't tell you more,' she said urgently. 'But this time you must trust me. We could both be killed if you don't. I promise to explain everything later.'

'Hey, Gloria,' Walt called from where he was unsaddling the horses, 'Stop flirting with our prisoner and give your loving husband a hand here.'

She hurried away leaving Luke more than a little puzzled. His captors were divided on some issue but he did not know what or how it would affect them. Gloria obviously knew something but how far could he trust her? It was hard to choose the lesser of two evils when the options themselves were still obscure.

15

The desert temperature dropped rapidly when the sun went down and the small amount of wood that they had was scarcely enough to heat some canned beans to add a little flavour to the single, hard-tack biscuit that Pierce allowed the other members of the group.

Conversation was limited and even without Gloria's warning Luke could sense that there was discord in the party. No arguments or harsh words were exchanged but the friendly discussions usually brought on by a campfire were noticeably absent. Everyone seemed to be deep in thought and spoke only when necessary.

There was no feed or water for the horses and they stood hollow-flanked and miserable on the picket line. If ridden carefully they would last another day but some of the inferior types might fail before that day was over.

Pierce stood up and strolled across to the smouldering remnants of the fire. He took a piece of paper from his pocket, held it up for the others to see and dropped it into the embers where it burst into flames. 'I won't be needing this map any more,' he announced and tapped a temple with his index finger, 'It's all in my head now.'

Luke realized immediately that the deserter was ensuring his own survival. If anything happened to him they would not find Murdering Wells and all would die in the desert. He knew too that they must be close to the water; when they reached it his usefulness would be ended. It would be unrealistic to think that Pierce would bother to take a wounded enemy any further. He had to get a gun before they reached the wells if he was to have any chance of survival.

The sand upon which he rested was growing cold and Luke asked Pierce, 'What about throwing my slicker over to me. You have it there with my saddle and saddle-bags.'

The deserter was stowing Matt's ivory-handled gun in the saddle-bag. He was out of ammunition for it and had placed his Army Colt back in his holster. He considered the request, judged it was harmless enough and tossed the oilskin coat across.

Luke spread the coat out, rolled on to it and began to drag a sweaty saddle blanket over himself for a cover. It would be little protection against the biting cold of the desert night but it was better than nothing.

'Not so fast,' Pierce growled as he saw his prisoner's preparations. He took a spare lariat and cut off a piece. 'Cover him, Walt,' he ordered, 'while I tie our friend up for the night.' To Luke he said, 'We don't want you playing any tricks while we are sleeping.'

'There's not a lot I could do with this leg the way it is.'

'It pays to be certain. Now put your hands behind you.'

'I can't sleep with my hands tied behind my back,' Luke protested.

'Don't worry. You'll be able to enjoy watching the stars. In fact if you don't do as you're told, you could start seeing a few stars any second from now.'

There was no point in arguing so Luke allowed Pierce to bind his hands behind his back. As he lay back and tried to sleep he was cold, thirsty, and his wounded leg was paining. What looked like being his last night on earth promised to be an uncomfortable one.

His bed was a fair way from the others and Luke could not hear the softly spoken conversations but gradually the others fell silent as sleep claimed them. He struggled with his bonds but Pierce had tied him securely. His efforts to get free shook the blanket off him and being unable to retrieve it he had only more discomfort to add to what certainly promised to be a miserable night.

Luke could only guess that he had been shivering and aching for a couple of hours when he saw a figure moving silently towards him. He was about to speak when he saw that it was Gloria. Seconds later a soft hand went over his mouth and her voice whispered, 'Shsh.'

He could smell her perfume as she whispered in his ear. 'I'm here to help. Don't make a sound. Roll over but do it quietly or we could both be dead.'

Under the circumstances Luke knew that it would be to his advantage to do as he was told. As quietly as he could, he rolled on to his face.

There was a tug at his bonds and he felt Gloria sawing at the ropes with a none-too-sharp knife. Completely mystified but with hopes surging, he made no sound for fear that his escape attempt would be detected. Then suddenly the ropes gave and his hands were free. He would have sat up but she gently pushed him back. 'Not yet,' Gloria whispered. She pressed a small revolver into his hand. 'Hide this where you can get at it quickly in the morning. I'll pretend to tie your hands again but will leave the rope loose so you can slip out of it. Listen to me. Sandy and Walt have decided to kill you and me. They intend to keep Pierce alive so he can steer them to the wells and tell them where he hid the loot from the job he did in New York. I overheard them plotting. They didn't know I was behind the horses in the dark. They have planned to make their move when we are saddling the horses. Sandy intends to shoot you where you are. Walt will cover Pierce and me. They'll take Pierce prisoner but Walt intends to kill me.'

'But you're his wife,' Luke whispered. 'Surely he wouldn't kill you?'

'Whatever was between us ended a long time ago. He forced me to come on this Western trip. I didn't want to get mixed up in criminal activities. I wanted to stay in New York. He is after Pierce's loot and has no intention of sharing it with a wife. Originally he needed me to divert suspicion. Everyone thinks kindly of a couple of young newlyweds just starting their life together.' She continued, speaking softly

174

and urgently. 'Keep an eye on Sandy tomorrow. When he moves close to shoot you, I'll scream. That's the only warning you'll get. Don't miss or we're both dead.'

'But what about Pierce? What is he going to do?'

'He's out of ammunition for that white-handled gun of your brother's and only has a couple of cartridges for the revolver he brought with him from the army. Sandy has refused to loan him any bullets to fit the other gun. He doesn't want Pierce to be able to do much fighting back. That's why we need your help. You are our life insurance.'

A dozen questions were in Luke's mind but Gloria risked discovery every second she remained talking to him. Before he could whisper any enquiries she left as silently as she had approached.

Luke was both relieved and puzzled. His mind was racing as he sought to comprehend his good fortune. Many questions would have to remain unanswered. As far as he was concerned the gun in his hand was evidence of good faith. By feel, he opened the loading gate, put the weapon on half-cock and rotated the cylinder. He could feel the brass cartridge heads and knew that it was loaded.

Pierce's role was still obscure but Luke would worry about that after disposing of the most immediate threat. Gloria did not seem to be worrying about him although he would certainly have an important role to play. He had always known that there would be trouble ahead but with his hands free and a loaded gun his chances of survival had improved greatly.

The rest of the night passed slowly and painfully. It was cold and sleep was out of the question. His wounded leg defied all Luke's efforts to get any degree of comfort. His mind was still struggling to comprehend the latest change in his fortune. Gloria's sudden change of heart had totally confused him. Had she changed sides? To his mind, whatever the day brought could not come soon enough.

It quickly became apparent that none of the others had slept very well either, for all left their blankets at first light.

The camp was a cheerless one with no wood for a fire and not even a decent breakfast. All were thirsty and his captors drank sparingly from their canteens but none considered the prisoner. Luke had not expected that they would. He refrained from asking for water, though. In a short time he expected that he would either be able to help himself, or he would be dead.

When Pierce awoke he started saddling his horse. Gloria did the same. This did not strike Sandy as being unusual because cavalry in the field always saddled up before eating. Walt was not in the habit but he saw no significance in what the others were doing. To him it was just another mundane job that could wait. He stood up, stretched and looked about, then stooped down and picked up his gun in its shoulder holster.

Luke had freed his hands and, with the revolver held behind his back, fixed his attention on Walt and Sandy. The former had not drawn his gun but it was in his hand; the latter had his hand in easy reach of his holster. Pierce and Gloria were partly hidden behind the horses. He found himself watching Sandy, who seemed the more dangerous of the pair. He knew that Walt was competent with a gun but it was Sandy's shooting that had led to his capture, so he made the young deserter his main target.

Gloria had started leading the two horses away before Walt noticed that something was amiss. 'Where are you going?' he called to his wife.

She gave an indistinct reply and continued walking.

Sandy was more curious than alarmed and walked closer to Luke to see around the other horses.

Luke was watching the young deserter, so he did not see what had made Gloria scream but it was the prearranged danger signal. He heard a shot, glimpsed Walt staggering and saw Sandy go for his gun. Throwing aside the blanket he brought up the little revolver. Other shots were registering on his consciousness but he only had eyes for the nearest deserter who was turning towards him as his gun cleared leather.

The little gun in Luke's hand barked once. Sandy reeled under the impact of the bullet but did not go down. He staggered towards the man who had shot him and raised the gun in his hand.

Luke fired again and the deserter fell forward on his face, almost on top of him. He moaned and moved slightly but was certainly out of the fight. Pierce was still firing. Where was Walt?

Glancing to the side, Luke saw Hammond stretched lifeless on the ground. Then a bullet kicked up the dirt beside him and he saw Pierce aiming his Army Colt for another shot. He had been double-crossed.

16

Luke pointed his gun at Pierce and squeezed the trigger but the hammer fell with a dull, muffled report. Ignoring the pain from his wounded leg, he rolled sideways, cursing the misfire. Hoping that a bullet was not stuck in the barrel, he fired again, another dull report but at least the gun did not blow up. Seeing the deserter about to try another shot, he rolled sideways again. The movement proved fortunate because Pierce's next shot struck right where he had been lying and it also brought him in reach of his own gun that Sandy had dropped. He snatched up the familiar weapon and to his surprise saw that the deserter was fleeing. He was already at long revolver range and Luke was aiming high in an attempt to hit him when a rifle bullet ploughed into the dirt beside him. As he rolled into a slight depression in the ground he glimpsed Gloria holding a pair of horses and cranking shots at him from his own carbine. Again he was fortunate. The girl was unfamiliar with a rifle and the horses she was holding were jerking nervously on the reins, upsetting her aim. Her intentions, though, were unmistakable. She was trying her best to kill him.

Pierce had already emptied his revolver and was almost back to where Gloria stood.

Reasoning that the deserter would take the rifle and that he could be expected to be a better shot because of his military training, Luke looked for more substantial cover. He saw a slightly deeper hollow in the ground near where Walt and Sandy had dropped their saddles. He rolled into the depression just as Pierce took the rifle from Gloria and fired a shot that hummed past his head.

Luke knew that he was still in trouble. The deserter was out of effective revolver range and had the advantage of a rifle. Then he saw Sandy's Spencer carbine lying just near his saddle. He threw himself forward, snatched the weapon and rolled back to cover as another rifle shot narrowly missed him. The sudden movement sent a shaft of pain through his wounded leg but he ignored it. The rifle could save his life.

Now, he thought, I can hit back. Throwing the weapon to his shoulder, he cocked the hammer, took a quick sight and squeezed the trigger. The firing-pin fell on an empty chamber. Suspecting it had been left that way for safety reasons, he worked the trigger guard to bring a cartridge from the magazine in the butt and cocked the big hammer again.

'He has a rifle,' Gloria called in alarm.

'It's one of the Spencers,' Pierce said urgently. 'Those guns have more range and power than this Winchester. Get on your horse and lead mine back behind that hill. We can't afford to have a horse hit.'

'What if he takes a shot at me?'

'He won't. I'll keep him busy. Anyway, he's too dumb to shoot at a lady even if he's now having a few doubts that you are one.'

Luke saw Gloria trot away with the horses but his main interest was in Pierce. The latter had sprinted to a couple of boulders that afforded him a fair degree of cover. He had tried to catch the deserter as he ran across to the rocks but found that his rifle was empty. For safety's sake, Sandy had been carrying it unloaded. For the second time that morning, Luke had been caught with an empty gun. He was sure that Sandy would have a few loose cartridges in his pocket but the dead deserter was at least five yards away and was lying in the open. Hindered by his wounded leg, Luke had little chance of reaching the body before being shot down.

A bullet from Pierce's rifle kicked up

dirt about a foot in front of his position. His enemy had not quite found his target but had the luxury of time to practise.

He remembered that the deserters had three military carbines. He had one and one was on the horse that Gloria was riding. One more was in the camp but he had no idea where, and Pierce certainly would not give him time to look for it. Trusting that the deserter still was not used to the Winchester, Luke peered above his shelter and looked about. A saddle was in reach and he dragged it towards him, thinking to use it as additional protection. Then he saw the missing rifle. It was propped against Walt Hammond's saddle but, given Luke's lack of mobility, he felt that it was an impossible distance away. The lariat attached to the saddle that partly sheltered him gave him an idea. If he could rope the carbine he could pull it towards him. That was, provided that Pierce's shooting did not improve in the meantime.

Eagerly he detached the rope and uncoiled it. The cavalry lariat was limp, soft rope and badly kinked from being carried in a tight coil. It would be hard to throw but the target was an easy one. Quickly he fashioned a noose and tried a quick round-arm throw. The loop missed but so did the shot that Pierce threw at him. He tried again. This time the rope went over the rifle barrel but failed to catch on anything and slipped off again. Another bullet buzzed past his ear. The deserter's aim was getting better and he would not miss for ever.

A third throw caught on something and the noose tightened. Cautiously Luke pulled and the rifle fell to the ground. Hand over hand, he started reeling in the rope while keeping under cover. With the weapon flat on the ground there was no chance of snagging it again if the rope slipped off. Fortunately it had caught over the big musket-type hammer and it held as Luke dragged the carbine to where he sheltered. The Spencer was covered in dirt from being dragged. Consequently the action was fouled and might fail to function, but the other carbine was relatively clean. He opened the butt trap, took out the magazine tube and tipped out five short, thick, rim-fire rounds. The breech was empty but five cartridges were a big improvement on none. As he fed the bullets into the other Spencer's butt, Luke was feeling more confident. He decided that under the circumstances he could afford to waste one shot just to let Pierce know that the odds against him were now greater.

When a big lead bullet whined off the rock that sheltered him, the deserter knew it was time to go. He broke cover and made a zigzag run up the ridge behind him.

Luke sent another shot after him but, being hampered by his wounded leg, lacked the freedom of movement necessary for snap shooting. Reluctant to waste any more precious cartridges, he could only watch in frustration as

Pierce disappeared over the crest. He reappeared briefly on the skyline and at first Luke thought he intended to engage in a long-range rifle duel, but the deserter had other plans.

He fired into the horses standing nervously on the picket line. By putting the remaining horses out of action, he prevented Luke from pursuing him or from escaping from the desert.

Horses are big animals and the .44 rim-fire cartridge was not a particularly powerful round. As the bullets thudded into them, one of the stricken animals went down immediately. Another staggered, and threw up its head while the third grunted in pain and shock. The fourth one sunk to its haunches. Just to be sure, Pierce shot each animal again. They were easy targets and he heard the bullets hitting them. This time two more of his targets went down. The fourth was swaying on its feet.

Not much of the deserter showed on the ridge, just a head and shoulders and rifle. Enraged, Luke fired another shot but had miscalculated the range and the bullet raised the dust just in front of his target. Satisfied that he was safe from pursuit and not wishing to chance a wound, Pierce rolled back behind the ridge and walked down to where Gloria waited with the horses.

She asked, 'Did you get him, Billy?'

Pierce took Lawyer's reins from her. 'No. I didn't get him but he has a wounded leg, no horses and no water. He won't be going anywhere and as he dies slowly of thirst he'll have plenty of time to think of how you played him for a sucker again — him and that useless husband of yours.'

When he was satisfied that his enemies were gone, Luke struggled to his feet and limped over to the wounded horses. Three were dead and the fourth stood in dumb agony. It could not be saved. To end its sufferings he shot the animal. After it fell he stood there, more enraged by Pierce's callous action than fearful of his situation. That would come later.

188

17

'We've done it,' Gloria laughed in relief. 'I'm rid of that no-good husband, Luke can't follow us and now it's plain sailing to Mexico.'

Pierce was not quite as enthusiastic. 'Don't celebrate too soon. We won't be going anywhere if we can't find those wells.'

'But surely nothing can go wrong now? You remember the map and according to that, the wells are just at the foot of that big column of rocks that we can see over there on the horizon. So far everything on the map has proved to be right. I think you are worrying too much.'

The deserter frowned. 'This is life-and-death stuff. It's not like New York. This country can kill you real quick. If Henry was lying or made a mistake somewhere, we could still be finished. I won't relax until I see that water. We're down to the last couple of mouthfuls in this canteen.' To emphasize his statement, Pierce lifted the canteen hanging from his saddle horn and shook it.

Lawyer needed little incentive to buck at any time and that one indiscreet move reminded him that he had not played his old tricks for several days. He snorted, reefed down his head and launched himself into a high, twisting buck.

Pierce was still aboard when the horse came down but only just. He had lost a stirrup and had lurched to one side. He had no chance of getting back into the centre of the saddle before Lawyer put in a low, spinning buck and again launched himself skywards. The rider made a frantic grab for the saddle horn, missed and tumbled back over the horse's quarters. He hit the ground solidly but was more alarmed than hurt. He knew that it could be disastrous to lose a horse.

'Catch him!' he screamed to Gloria. 'Don't let him get away.'

The woman tried but she had never caught a runaway animal in her life and, like everyone unfamiliar with the task, she proceeded to chase and try to catch it rather than work wide and eventually head it off. Lawyer had too much speed for Gloria's mount and rapidly increased the distance between them. His task was made easier because Pierce was used to the joined reins of the cavalry and had knotted together Luke's unjoined ones. The reins that should have been under the horse's feet and hampering his progress were still on his neck.

Fearful that Gloria would exhaust their one remaining horse, Pierce was forced to admit defeat. He bellowed, 'Let the sonofabitch go. Don't run the guts out of your horse.'

By this time the girl was out of earshot, but eventually she reached the same conclusion. Lawyer had too much speed to catch. She rode back to where

Pierce waited, her pony lathered in sweat and its head drooping with weariness.

By then the deserter's anger had been replaced by fear. It was just possible that they would safely reach the wells but if anything went wrong before they did, circumstances could quickly turn fatal.

★ ★ ★

Luke hobbled about the deserted camp using a carbine as a walking-stick. Rummaging through Walt's belongings, he found another clean shirt which he tore into strips and set about dressing the wound in his leg. It was no worse but no better and he knew that infection could set in if the injury was not promptly and properly treated.

He had no intention of waiting patiently in the desert to die of thirst. Although he had been about eighteen hours without water and had more than a day's walk back to Barrel Creek, he was determined not to give in. He found a can of beans among the abandoned supplies and butchered the can open with a jack knife that Sandy had been carrying. The sauce from the can was thick but it was liquid and would help a bit. He ate the beans too, because he would need all the strength he could get. There were also a couple of cans of sardines that he placed in his pockets. He was not sure whether the fish and the oil they were in would help or exacerbate his thirst. When he was sure he had nothing to lose, he would open the cans. His wounded leg was painful and he could only hope that it would loosen up as he walked.

It was not the best time of the day to be walking in the desert but he could find no shelter from the sun and was determined to walk while he could. Although walking in the sun was damaging, he feared that the leg might stiffen if he waited until dark and by then he would be so much thirstier.

Sooner or later, Luke was sure that

Lawyer would unload Pierce but the horse would not head back to Barrel Creek if it could get water at Murdering Wells. Throwing a rider and escaping later were two different things and the long, unjoined reins on his bridle were designed to keep a riderless horse from running away. He could not count on Lawyer coming back over his tracks although the possibility existed.

Step by painful step, Luke forced himself along. Even fully fit, the journey would have been a daunting one. Though he prayed for sunset, the sun seemed to hang in the sky and concentrate its heat on the man struggling below. When he came to a patch of shade cast by a tall boulder or a high ridge he would halt and rest, but when he did a voice in his mind seemed to whisper, *Give up, it's hopeless*.

18

'Billy, my feet are getting sore,' Gloria complained. 'How much further do I have to walk?'

Pierce, who trudged beside her said, 'It's only a mile or so now. We have to save this horse because it has to get us to Mexico. Once it's had a good drink you'll be able to do a lot more riding. We will have to nurse the horse along but it should last the distance if we are careful.'

Gloria could feel the sun's intensity as it seemed to drain the energy from her body. 'I didn't think it would be like this. It all sounded so easy in your letters. Walt and I were to get you away from the army, you would get rid of Walt and we would live happily ever after on the money you got from that big job in New York. Where is that money, Billy?'

'I'll tell you when the time's right. This all would have been easy if Luke Adison hadn't stuck his nose into things. I hope he's really suffering now. At least we had a good drink before we left camp. We thought we could use him but he spoiled things again.'

'Don't blame me. I persuaded him to help us get rid of the others. You were the one who wanted me to give him my gun.'

Pierce was not in the mood for criticism. 'It was a good idea,' he insisted. 'Giving him two live rounds and putting doctored shells in the other chambers would have kept him from harming us if it hadn't been for bad luck. He did what we needed him to do and put Sandy out of action. How was I to know that the useless sonofabitch would fall near him and he would be able to get another gun? I can't think of every possibility and I can't undo what's happened, so I have to play the cards as they fall. We're still ahead in this game and once we hit Mexico we'll be in clover. This is the hardest part just now, but we can survive. In a few days you'll have forgotten this.'

Gloria shook her head. 'I'll remember this till the day I die.'

Pierce laughed and pointed at a clump of trees at the base of the rocks in the distance. 'That day will be a long time coming. The wells are in those trees. We can rest up overnight, soak up plenty of water and it should be plain sailing to Mexico. I can arrange to get the money from there and then it's a life of ease for the pair of us. You went through a lot for me, Gloria, but it will pay off now.'

* * *

Luke had plenty of time to think as he struggled along. He felt foolish that originally he had been taken in so easily. You should know better, he reproached himself as he walked; a pretty girl smiles at you and you believe everything she says. No wonder you are in this fix.

If Sandy had not been one of his brother's deserters, he would have felt bad about shooting him as he had allowed himself to be used in a situation very much like murder. The two live cartridges and the remaining empty shells in Gloria's gun had been no oversight. It had been a simple matter to pull the lead from the cartridges and empty out the powder charge. The primers in the empty shells would still fire but were harmless. Pierce had used Luke as a means of reducing the odds against him while denying him protection when he was no longer needed. It was only luck that Sandy's gun had fallen within reach, otherwise Pierce would have killed him as well. The plan had been absolutely ruthless and had almost worked. He wondered whether Gloria or Pierce had engineered the double-cross. The woman had gone along with it and played her part well but did she really know what Pierce had been planning? Walt and Sandy had been fooled completely and Gloria had played her part so well that he had almost trusted her again. Given more time he might have been able to do something different but it had all happened so quickly.

It hurt to think of the two plotters escaping and Luke was determined to survive so that he could track them down later. He would not count the miles or the hours but would keep moving towards safety as long as it was physically possible for him to do so. He promised himself that somehow he would survive. Somehow he would go to Mexico and start his quest for the pair.

The heat and thirst were taking their toll but his wounded leg was his biggest worry. If it deteriorated to the extent that he could not walk, all hope was gone.

The shadows were getting longer and his strength was waning. Following the hoof-tracks was easy in daylight but night would bring the added worry of going astray. He could not afford to cover any extra distance. Though it seemed unlikely that he would survive the journey ahead of him, self-preservation and the urge for revenge were providing powerful motivation.

Just as the sun was going down he happened to glance behind him and caught a sign of distant movement. The glare of the sunset and the long shadows were playing tricks with the light and he had to change his position and pull his hat-brim lower before he could discern that the object of his attention was a horse. The animal was walking briskly and the last of the sunlight caught its yellowish coat. 'Lawyer,' he called. 'Over here, boy.'

The animal lifted its head and neighed in recognition.

19

It seemed ages before the two people and their horse reached the trees at the base of the rocky spire. Viewed across open desert the place had looked closer than it really was. Both were sore-footed, almost at the end of their endurance, parched by their exertions and the relentless sun. They had mostly walked, trying to save the horse as much as possible for without it there was only a very slim chance that they could reach Mexico. At best it was a fairly ordinary animal; now it presented a miserable sight as it plodded along, with hollows in its flanks and its hair matted by large patches of dried sweat.

The pair halted at the trees. 'I can't walk another step,' Gloria said as she threw herself down in the shade. She looked about. 'I don't see any wells.' A note of urgency came into her voice.

'Where are they, Billy? I can't see them.'

'You won't,' Pierce told her. 'They are just two holes in the ground but, according to Henry, someone put rocks around them so they would be easy to find and folks would not walk down them in the dark.'

He took the empty canteen from the saddle. 'I'll find the wells and bring you back a drink. Just rest there.'

'I hope they're not too deep, Billy. We forgot to take the bucket from the camp. How will we water the horse?'

Pierce frowned. 'That ruckus in camp spoiled everything. I never thought of the bucket. We were lucky to get out as well as we did.'

'You call this getting out well?' Gloria said bitterly through sun-cracked lips. 'Hurry up and get that water. You might need to water the horse from your hat and that will take time.'

'Don't remind me. A horse can drink five gallons at a time and raising that much water and putting it into a hat bit by bit is going to take a lot of time.'

'The horse can wait, Billy. I can't. Hurry up and find those wells.

★ ★ ★

It was with great relief that Luke saw the horse turn towards him, but doubts came flooding in to haunt him. What if the animal refused to be caught? Would he be able to ride if he did catch it?

A glance at Lawyer's hollow flanks showed that he had been many hours without a drink. This meant that he had escaped from Pierce before reaching Murdering Wells. A horse that thirsty would not venture away from the water. Luke called again and, much to his relief, the animal gave a friendly snuffle as it walked up to where he waited.

'So you got rid of Pierce, eh? I hope you broke the sonofabitch's neck when you unloaded him. But if you try the same trick with me, I'll skin you alive.'

Despite all his confident talk, Luke was not sure that he would still be able to ride. Certainly he could not mount by the stirrup. If he failed to get into the saddle, he had no chance of surviving.

He looked around and after some moments he saw a shallow erosion ditch, cut by rain water over the centuries. It took a while to get the horse into position in the little gully but eventually he was able to stand on the bank and ease his wounded leg across the saddle. When he found the offside stirrup his leg throbbed painfully. He tried leaving the foot out of the stirrup but the pain was even worse. As he turned the animal back toward Barrel Creek, Luke knew that a long ordeal lay ahead. Also he doubted that he would be able to get back on Lawyer if he was forced to dismount. The creek was many miles ahead and he could only hope that the horse could complete the journey. It was into its second day without water. The buckskin was tough, he knew that, but the animal had seen some hard usage.

Night was falling but he no longer feared missing the tracks of the previous day. Even if the horse was too far away to smell the water, it knew where it was and would take the shortest possible way to get there. Regardless of how badly he felt, Luke knew that his survival now depended upon his ability to stay in the saddle and the horse's strength to keep going.

Lawyer no longer had his customary, long-striding walk and possibly he was not carrying his head quite so high but he forged ahead as the sun's glare left the landscape at last and a cooler darkness descended.

Luke clung to reins and saddle horn, trying hard to ignore his thirst and the pain from his wounded leg. The situation was still grim but having a horse under him brought back the hope that he had almost lost.

* * *

Pierce found the larger of the two wells first. If it had not been for the stones around the edge, he might well have walked into it in the darkness. With a sigh of relief, he dropped to his knees and peered down the hole. No gleam of water met his eye and he could see only blackness. Feeling about he found a stone and dropped it in. A dull thud came back. The well was dry.

Thankful that there was another well in the area he climbed to his feet and continued his quest.

Gloria called. 'Have you found the wells yet?'

'I found one but it's dry. There's another one around here somewhere,' the deserter shouted back. He continued his search pushing through bushes and peering into the pools of darkness caused by the shadows that the rising moon was starting to throw.

Eventually he kicked a stone and, by feeling around, found others arranged in a circular pattern. He picked up a stone and dropped it into the dark hole before him. No splash came back, just a dry thud as the rock hit bare earth. The sound made Pierce's blood freeze. He had found the wells but both were dry. He struck a match and dropped it down the hole but could detect no gleam of water.

His mind was trying to reject the information that the wells were dry. Such a thing could not be. But another voice seemed to cut through the mental panic, a cold voice that told him: you're dead.

'Billy — hurry up. I'm awfully dry.'

There was no easy way to break the news and in his present state the deserter was not in a mood to spare anyone's feelings. 'I've found two wells but they're both dry.'

'They can't be. There has to be water here.'

Pierce tried to sound casual although panic was threatening to swamp his reasoning. 'Maybe there's others. I'll keep looking. There's a fair bit of brush around here. I might be able to find water in the morning when I can see better.'

'I can't wait till morning. I'm dying

of thirst. I can't stand another six or seven hours of this.'

'You have no choice, Gloria. So get used to it. I don't like this situation any better than you do but lying around complaining won't help anyone. We have to wait till morning.'

There was real fear in the woman's voice. 'Billy — We're going to die here.'

'Not if I can help it,' he muttered.

The deserter saw no point in telling Gloria that he was forming another plan. But this time she would not be involved.

The horse was standing where they had left it. The cool night air might have revived it slightly and if it had any travel left in it, now was the time to go. The risk was a calculated one but it seemed to be the only option.

He walked to the horse and un-cinched the saddle, which he carried over and dropped beside the woman. 'When the sweat dries out of this saddle blanket, it will keep you warm. There's a bit of grub in the saddlebags if you're hungry. I'm just going to give the horse a rubdown. If we can't find water in the morning, it might just be able to get us to the next water.'

'Do you really think it could?' A note of hope crept back into Gloria's voice.

'There's a good chance,' he told her. 'My pals in the cavalry used to say that a horse can go three days without water if it's ridden properly.'

Pierce was staking all that the animal they had was capable of such a feat and, to be sure, he was reducing the amount of weight on its back. The saddle, saddlebags and rifle would account for at least fifty pounds and the reduced weight might just be enough to improve his chances.

'What are we going to do?' The despair in Gloria's voice was evident. 'You have to get us out of this, Billy. Walt and I risked everything for you.'

Pierce vigorously rubbed the horse's back to break up the dried sweat. 'Don't worry about a thing. I've got something figured out.' With that, he vaulted on to the horse's bare back.

'Billy? What are you doing?'

He turned the horse's head toward the south. Though he knew he would not be believed, he was past caring. 'I'm going for help,' he announced.

Gloria screamed. She had not expected such a betrayal. 'Wait. Don't leave me here. Come back!'

Pierce ignored her and kicked the horse into a reluctant trot. It was not very fast but too fast for the exhausted woman to follow.

Anger replaced fear and shock, Gloria snatched the discarded carbine from its saddle scabbard. 'Come back!'

He ignored her.

She fired then, spraying wild shots after the man who was leaving her to die. All missed him but one struck the horse in the hindquarters. It snorted and kicked but responded when the rider urged it into a canter.

★　★　★

The buckskin horse plodded along guided by its instincts to its last memory of water. Its rider clung to the saddle horn, parched and in agony from his injured leg. Luke had no idea how long they had been travelling when suddenly the black shape of a mountain range loomed in his path.

'Keep going, old buddy,' he mumbled to Lawyer. 'Barrel Creek's just over those mountains.'

The horse started to climb the slope, sometimes walking, sometimes plunging up steep sections where a bit more speed was needed. Luke helped all he could by ensuring that he stayed balanced and kept his weight well forward where the horse could best handle it. It was hard to maintain the correct seat on the slope and his injured leg registered a painful protest, but he knew that he could not get to the water without the horse and that careless riding would throw his weight out of balance and increase the strain on Lawyer.

They were nearing the crest of the range when the horse stumbled to its knees. For one horrible moment, Luke thought that the animal had at last given out. But it had merely missed its step and knew that the water was not far ahead. Regaining all fours it stood there with its sides heaving while it rested from its exertions. Much to its rider's relief the buckskin, a short time later, continued the struggle to the top. It halted again on the summit to get its breath again.

Luke leaned forward and patted the sweaty neck. 'The hard part is behind us now. Just don't fall over on the way down to the creek.'

The descent seemed to take for ever, but then Luke heard the sound of water trickling over rocks. Barrel Creek and safety were just ahead.

20

Pierce might have travelled five miles from Murdering Wells when his wounded horse finally collapsed. His first emotion was rage that the animal should collapse when it was needed so much. But then fear took over. Dismounted, parched and faccd by miles of desert, he abandoned all hope of survival. Resignation, though, brought no peace and doubts started to torture him. He wondered whether he had not been too hasty in abandoning his search for another well. There might have been another one somewhere in the brush.

His instinct for survival told him to return to the wells and search again in daylight, but dawn was breaking and although he could see the column of rocks in the distance, the walk seemed to be beyond him. Gloria had a rifle and would most likely shoot him on sight before he had a chance to concoct some excuse to explain his actions. In desperation Pierce began to retrace his steps. He was getting weaker and it took him nearly an hour to cover the first mile. Then the sun came up and searing heat replaced the night chill.

His mouth was dry, his lips cracked and his tongue swollen, but that did not prevent him from venting his anger and shouting his defiance at the empty desert. He croaked out curses on everything and everyone whom he considered had brought him to such a hopeless situation. His greatest anger, though, was directed at the Murdering Wells. At last he gave way to his fears and threw himself down in the sand, still cursing and raving at the injustice of his predicament.

He was close enough to hear the shot as Gloria ended her life, but if he did hear it, the sound did not register in his thirst-tortured brain.

★ ★ ★

Luke resisted the urge to drink too deeply but allowed Lawyer to take on a fair amount of water. The horse still had a lot more travelling to do and it would take a long time to restore the moisture sweated from its system. At the first decent patch of grass he halted, allowed the horse another drink from the creek, unsaddled it, rubbed its back and then staked it out to graze. He stretched out on the soft grass, opened a can of sardines and hungrily devoured them. He was still hungry and was debating eating the remaining can when, despite the pain of his wound, he fell asleep.

The noonday heat woke him. It was a struggle to get to his feet but he limped to the creek, stretched out on the bank and drank deeply. Then he took Lawyer for another drink and staked him out on a fresh patch of grass. The last can of sardines was quickly eaten. Then it was time to consider resuming his journey. The water, food and rest had helped greatly but, if anything his wounded leg was getting sorer.

It was a major effort to saddle his horse and again Luke was forced to find a piece of sloping ground so that he could mount more easily. Once mounted, he allowed the horse to have another drink. Then he started following the course of the creek. They were getting into the vicinity of Coterill's hidden cabin when he saw movement in the trees ahead.

Though he had no reason to expect trouble, Luke's hand strayed to the butt of his Colt. So much had happened in the past couple of days that he was not prepared to take chances.

A rider emerged from the trees, a big man on a solid bay horse. He was looking at the tracks that the Pierce party had made. Lawyer snorted and when the stranger looked up in alarm, Luke saw it was Shadrach Payne, Sheriff Stone's deputy. Behind him other riders were appearing from among the trees.

The deputy reined in his mount. 'Luke Adison,' he said in surprise.

216

'What are you doing here?'

'I could ask you the same question, Shadrach, but I expect you'll tell me soon enough. I'm just escaping from the last of those army deserters and the not-so-tender clutches of Gloria Hammond and her latest boyfriend who is using the name of Billy Pearce.'

Another rider joined them. It was Marshal Slattery, wearing his usual sour expression. He glowered at Luke and rasped, 'I told you to stay out of this matter, Adison. You are interfering with a government investigation, and if any of that gang escape I will hold you responsible.'

'There aren't many of that gang left, Marshal, except an army deserter calling himself Pierce and a lady who was in cahoots with him. She was an old criminal acquaintance of Pierce's from New York. Her husband Walt was with them too but she had him killed out there in the desert. I was lucky enough to escape.'

Slattery growled. 'I think you had

better tell us what you know. I was originally sent here to investigate an organization dealing in government property purchased from deserters. Then I received word that one deserter was wanted over a big robbery in New York. When I eventually got to close the net I found nothing but dead bodies. You have a bit of explaining to do.'

Luke recounted the events as he recalled them. Slattery, Shadrach Payne and a couple of lawmen who had not been introduced, crowded around to hear what had happened. Occasionally the marshal would ask a question but mostly just sat sour-faced on his horse and interrupted as little as possible. At last he said, 'So Pierce and Gloria Hammond are still alive?'

'They were last I saw of them. They only had one horse between them but were heading for Murdering Wells. Pierce had a map. He bought it from a kid who worked for Coterill. From what I could gather he was suspicious of the length of time Coterill was keeping them at the hideout. He knew exactly where to go but he kept it a secret from everyone else. If you hurry you might catch up with them before they get to Mexico.'

'We're not equipped for a journey into the desert. We have no water canteens and we could lose two days getting them and getting back here,' Slattery said. There was anger and frustration in his voice.

'But they'll get away,' Luke protested.

Shadrach contradicted him. 'No, they won't. From what you have told us they were not carrying much water. They won't get far past Murdering Wells. It's the old case of a little knowledge being dangerous.'

Slattery was in no mood to play guessing games. 'What are you talking about?'

But the deputy would not be hurried. He looked at the puzzled faces around him. 'Why do you think Coterill kept Pierce and the others at the hideout for so long?'

'I wouldn't have a clue,' the marshal snapped. 'Get on with your story. We don't have all day.'

'Coterill knew that Murdering Wells only held water for a few months after the rain in July. The rain did not come this July and he was not venturing out into the desert until there were a couple of good, heavy showers. It seems Pierce got too smart for his own good. Those wells are dry. That pair out there have no chance.'

'Do you know that for sure?' Luke asked. 'I thought there was some great secret about those wells.'

'Lots of folks around here know about those wells and their location but a bad legend has grown up around them and nobody goes there. Why should they? There's nothing out there. I've been there myself. I guided an army mapping team there in 'sixty seven and I've helped recover a body or two over the years. The real secret is that the wells only have water for a few months of the year. In the early days a lot of men relied on those wells and died. That's why they were called Murdering Wells. They killed so many who thought they could rely on them.'

'We have to get back there,' Luke said. 'Someone might still be alive by the time we get there. We can't just leave them to die.'

'They left you to die,' Slattery reminded him. 'But that idea also appeals to me so I won't hold that against them. As far as I'm concerned that pair got what was coming to them and I don't intend risking men's lives to recover a couple of bodies. Until the rain comes, the buzzards are welcome to them. When Shadrach Payne here knows that the wells are safe again I'm sure Sheriff Stone will send someone out to pick up what's left.'

Luke protested further but the marshal turned his horse around. 'We can continue this argument in Copper Rocks, but if you know what's good for you, you won't.'

Payne reined his horse in beside

Lawyer and said quietly. 'He's right Luke. By the time we could get a properly equipped posse out to the wells, Pearce and Gloria Hammond would surely be dead. I've seen it before. Folks with guns usually blow their brains out when they go mad with thirst. We can't do anything for them now.'

'I feel that we should at least try, Shadrach. It seems wrong to just leave them.'

'The decision isn't yours. You have to leave them. You can't ride back out there on your own and that wounded leg of yours needs fixing up. You could get blood poisoning and die or you might even lose your leg. You're coming back with me if I have to knock you out and sling you over a horse. So don't argue.'

Reluctantly Luke pointed Lawyer after the others, then said to the deputy, 'I guess you're right. I wonder what will happen now.'

'The case is closed. Though he don't

look it, Slattery is happy. He'll twist the facts into some sort of a report that makes this whole thing look like a smooth operation and the fuss will die down. Slattery will emerge a hero. I doubt that you will get much of a mention but it will save a few awkward questions being asked later.'

'I suppose I should be happy,' Luke said. 'In a way I've had my revenge and I even recovered Matt's gun. But I wish things had ended differently. I reckon that in future when folks talk about how cruel nature can be, I'll remember what happened here.'

'Nature ain't cruel. We get into trouble because we don't read the signs she shows us. Them wells didn't murder anyone. The ones who died there just didn't know enough about them.'

'You could be right about that. We might discuss this subject in greater depth over drinks in the saloon at Copper Rocks. I'll need to get this leg fixed up so I can ride properly again, so

I could be around for a while. Lawyer needs a bit of a rest too.'

'You wouldn't be interested in selling him by any chance?'

Luke stroked the tangled black mane. 'Many's the time I've cussed this horse, but money won't buy him. A man could go a whole lifetime and not find another as good. This horse saved my life yesterday. He's not perfectly behaved but I reckon I can trust him more than I could a woman.'

The deputy laughed. 'You won't say that when you meet the right one.'

'Maybe not. I'll just have to keep looking.'

THE END

Other titles in the
Linford Western Library:

BY THE GUN THEY DIED

Matt James

With seven killers camped on his trail, big Blaze Morgan rides south into Weeping Woman Valley. With his superior gun skills and horsemanship, Morgan expects that he will soon shake off his pursuers. But it's a dark and a stormy night and when he's violently thrown from his horse he finds that he will be lucky to survive the next twenty-four hours . . . Can he ever hope to overcome the obstacles in his way?